It's been said that if you love someone, set them free. If they come back they're yours; if they don't they never were. But what does it mean when they come back into your life—as your sibling's significant other?

At twenty-five years old, Cal Adams has only ever truly loved one man, the one who broke his heart three years earlier—Andrew Hall. Since then, he has searched for meaningful relationships but cannot smolder the flames of the past his family remains unaware of.

As the holiday season approaches, Cal's younger sister, Claire, brings her boyfriend home to meet the family. When she arrives, Cal is shocked to meet her boyfriend, who is none other than Andrew. In a darkly humorous tale, Cal decides to show his ex what he missed out on.

A FAMILY AFFAIR

Rob Loveless

A NineStar Press Publication

Published by NineStar Press
P.O. Box 91792,
Albuquerque, New Mexico, 87199 USA.
www.ninestarpress.com

A Family Affair

Printed in the USA
First Edition
April, 2020

Print ISBN: 978-1-951880-96-5

Also available in eBook, ISBN: 978-1-951880-93-4

Warning: This book contains sexually explicit content, which may only be suitable for mature readers, and infidelity.

Chapter One

Cal Adams sat at his desk and shuffled through some papers as he eyed the clock: 5:47 p.m. A mixture of excitement and anxiety churned uneasily in his stomach as the seconds hand ticked away. In thirteen minutes, he would relinquish his work responsibilities and prepare for what was sure to be a big night. A few days earlier, Cal's parents had called to invite him to dinner Friday night for a special occasion—his baby sister would be home from college for the weekend.

Claire Adams was a senior in college and only three and a half years younger than Cal, yet he couldn't help but refer to her as his baby sister; perhaps that was part of being a big brother. As Claire's older brother and only sibling, Cal was a bit on edge about that night's family dinner. After all, Claire wasn't just coming home to visit; she was bringing along her new boyfriend to meet the family.

Cal tuned out the clinking of weight machines and the grunts of fatigued gym patrons as he sat in his office and concentrated on the circumstance at hand. His sister hadn't had a boyfriend meet their parents since her junior year of high school, which meant this was serious. Cal and Claire had become very close in recent years, but he had not heard much about this boyfriend, including his name. Claire had always been one to maintain a low profile on social media, and only acknowledged she was "in a relationship" a month or so ago—without posting any photos. From what Cal had been able to gather from his phone calls with her, Claire and her boyfriend had only been seeing each other for about six months. So they hadn't been together that long. Still, this was serious, which worried Cal a bit.

Being the big brother, Cal was somewhat protective of his sister, but he was happy for Claire, and he was sure he'd love her boyfriend. After all, Claire had a good head on her shoulders. However, this whole situation made Cal uneasy since it made him reflect on his own lack of success in the relationship department.

As the elder sibling, Cal had always anticipated he would be the first to settle down. However, being twenty-five years old and never having been in a serious relationship, he often felt frustrated and unfulfilled—like something was missing in his life.

It wasn't that Cal was undateable. On the contrary, he was quite attractive, with medium-length, dark-brown hair, piercing gray eyes, sharp features, and a lean build. He was successful, independent, and had an easygoing, fun-loving personality. In fact, he went on plenty of dates, but nothing ever seemed to pan out. Either the chemistry wasn't there or things just didn't advance. Cal hadn't experienced genuine feelings for anyone since—

"Hey," a friendly voice chimed, which snapped Cal's attention back to work. A petite young woman with a pretty, freckled face and long, ginger tresses appeared at his office door.

"Hi, Sophie," Cal greeted. "Getting ready to head out?"

"Yeah, my six o'clock canceled on me," she informed him.

Sophie was a personal trainer at the gym Cal managed and also one of his closest friends. Sophie was a year his senior, and the two had been friends since childhood. They knew everything about each other's lives: the good, the not-so-good, and the bad.

Cal glanced at the clock: nearly six now. "I'll be leaving in a few too."

"Any fun weekend plans?" Sophie asked.

"Well, I have that family dinner tonight, but I'm not sure if I would call it fun."

"Ohh, that's right!" she said. "Claire's bringing home *the boyfriend*. What do you know about him?"

"Nothing," Cal replied. "Honestly, I don't even think my parents know much about him."

"So this is a pretty big deal," Sophie stated. "It sounds serious."

"Yeah, it does," he sighed with a lack of enthusiasm before he shut off his computer.

"Uh oh, sounds like someone's big brother senses are tingling," she teased.

"It's not that. I'm sure this guy is great. And I'm happy for Claire, I really am. But I'm twenty-five years old and—"

"Cal, you can't keep thinking like that. You're young, and you'll find someone."

"That's what all my friends say, but you guys are all in relationships," Cal countered. "You and Rich have been together for years."

"Believe me, you're gonna find someone. *Soon*. I'm sure of it," Sophie reassured him as she gave his arm a squeeze. "By the way, I forgot to ask, how did the date go with that guy last night?"

"Eh, it was fine...at first."

"At first?" she questioned.

"Yeah, I mean, he was cute. We just grabbed a coffee. And he seemed to have a good personality."

"So what happened?"

"He started talking about how he loves popping molly."

"No!"

"Oh yeah. And then he told me Lana Del Rey's music makes him horny. Those were his exact words."

"What!" Sophie gasped in disbelief. "He did not!"

"I'm telling you I can't make this stuff up," Cal chuckled as he shook his head in disbelief. "And really, Lana Del Rey? I didn't know melancholic songs could get someone all hot and bothered."

"You're such a normal guy. How come you always find these crazies?"

"I don't know, I guess they're drawn to me," he joked. "But, in all seriousness, I hate these stupid dating apps. I wish I didn't have to use them, but I don't know how else to meet someone. Every time I do meet someone from the apps though, they're crazy or—"

"Or you don't feel the spark."

"No. At least not like I had with—"

"Hey"—Sophie interrupted in a soft voice—"it's been over three years."

"I know. I know," Cal stated. He stood from his desk and grabbed his charcoal peacoat. "And I'm over it—believe me—I am. I just get scared that—"

"Don't be. You'll have those feelings again. You'll find that spark."

"Yeah, I know," he sighed with a slight shrug before he hit the lights and left his office with Sophie. The two exited the gym in silence and were soon embraced by the crisp air of late November.

"Hey, are you going to be okay?" Sophie finally asked. Cal could see misty wisps of breath swirl in front of her as she spoke.

"Yeah, I'm fine," he said. He had spent a great deal of time rehearsing that line to assure everyone—including himself—that he was, in fact, fine.

"All right. Well, I'm parked down the street. Let me know how tonight goes."

"I will," Cal replied before he began walking in the opposite direction toward his own car.

Cal hated when people asked if he was going to be okay. He knew he was going to be fine. No, he *was* fine...wasn't he? He had hit a little bump in the road a while ago, but he was back on his feet, and he was fine. Probably.

About three years earlier, Cal had encountered a bit of a rough patch. He had graduated college a semester early with honors and immediately received a job offer within his field from a prestigious corporation. Everyone thought he was on the fast track toward success, but Cal was miserable.

His job had required that he relocate hours away from his friends and family, which isolated him. Day in and day out, Cal went to work at a job he was never quite interested in and then came home to an empty apartment. Despite his amiable personality, Cal felt insecure and shy living in an unfamiliar town. As a result, he often retreated to his apartment which prevented him from being able to meet new people, and his coworkers were distant and standoffish. Cal felt an enormous pressure to meet everyone's expectations—at least, the expectations he assumed had been set for him—without regard for his own well-being. And to top it all off, Cal had gone through a bad breakup right before graduating and taking the job.

Well, technically, you can't break up with someone you were never really with.

He pulled his coat tight as he shuddered from a combination of the frigid weather and the thought of what could've been and what never was. A gust of icy wind slapped Cal's clean-shaven face before tiny snowflakes began to dance through the night sky, which indicated winter was approaching.

Cal had always loved the winter—he still did. But now as an adult, an irrational sense of dread accompanied it, probably because it reminded him of when he lost it all. Within a month of starting that job, Cal felt lost and alone as a result of relocating and began seeing a psychiatrist to treat him for depression.

Cal wanted to be happy and knew he had much to be thankful for: he was independent, graduated early, and had a job. Still, he couldn't help feeling *gray*. He knew that gray wasn't an actual emotion, but that's how Cal described his feelings to the shrink.

He grew more and more hopeless as each day passed. Every day, Cal came home from work and either wanted to bawl his eyes out or punch a hole in the wall of his dreary apartment; most days he did the former. His depression escalated to the point where he could no longer eat, and his already thin body soon became even more slight.

After eight lonely months, Cal finally realized he could not put his life on standby any longer. He had always been a rational person, which resulted in him putting practicality before his own happiness. He had taken this job not because he wanted to, but because he had been expected to. However, the time had come for Cal to reclaim his life.

After a particularly stressful day of work, Cal decided he'd had enough. He walked into his supervisor's office and quit his job abruptly, saying that he would not return the next day. Within a week, he packed up his apartment, and moved back home to live with his parents. Not the ideal postgrad scenario, but Cal knew it was necessary to his mental well-being. His parents were more than happy to have him home, especially since Claire had just moved several hours away to begin her freshman year of college in an area only a short distance from Cal's alma mater. Cal hadn't moved back to be coddled by his parents, but he just needed to be someplace where he could rebuild his life and focus on what he wanted.

One of the perks of moving back home was that Cal was able to reconnect with Sophie. Though the two had texted each other almost daily, he was able to see her on a regular basis. Sophie started bringing Cal to the gym where she worked and helped him get back in shape. Working out not only restored him to a healthy physique, but it also released endorphins which helped to alleviate his depression.

After a few months, Sophie heard of a job opening at the gym, and she encouraged Cal to apply for the position. Within a few days, he was interviewed, offered the job, and was able to put his business management degree to use. And two years later, here he was in the best shape of his life and employed at a job he loved. Prior to graduating, he would never have envisioned this to be his life, but now that it was, he was happy. He *was* fine.

Cal was grateful for the slight warmth provided by the concrete walls of the parking garage, which shielded him from the blustery winter gust, as he strode toward his car. He stepped into the aging vehicle, started its engine, and waited impatiently for the heat to kick in. Cal had owned this car since his freshman year of college, and it had seen better days. The vehicle's clunky body was marked with several scratches and the unimpressive silver paint was chipped in places. Still, it drove well, so Cal was unwilling to upgrade to a newer model just yet.

Snow flurries grew thicker as Cal pulled out of the parking garage. Fortunately his apartment was a short distance from the gym and the snow did not appear to be sticking to the ground. Cal arrived home just after 6:15 p.m. and hustled to get ready. His mother insisted on him arriving at seven o'clock sharp, and his childhood home was about twenty-five minutes away from his current apartment.

He slipped out of his business-casual work attire and pulled on a fashionable black sweater and a pair of dark-washed jeans. Then, he grabbed an unopened bottle of Merlot from the kitchen and headed out the door.

When he arrived at his parents' house, Cal parked his car in the driveway and took a deep breath to prepare himself for the evening ahead. He reminded himself that this was Claire's night and he should be happy for his younger sister instead of focusing on his own love life—or lack thereof. With one last calming inhale, he stepped out of the car.

As Cal approached the front door, he could hear metal pans clanking in the kitchen and muffled voices calling out from inside. He grasped the icy doorknob and paused for a moment before entering the house; this was it.

"Todd, are you in the bathroom?" Martha Adams shouted from the heated kitchen.

"What?" her husband's muffled voice responded from the second floor.

"I said are you in the bathroom?" she repeated louder. The scent of garlic and various roasted vegetables pervaded Cal's nostrils as he hung up his coat in the foyer. Upstairs, a door creaked open followed by his father's agitated voice which was much clearer now.

"For Christ's sake, Martha, I can't hear you. I'm in the bathroom!"

"All right, well that's what I was asking!" she hollered back over the sound of the oven door creaking open. "Come down when you're finished. I need your help." The bathroom door upstairs slammed shut.

"Hi, Mom," Cal greeted as he stepped into the kitchen, his presence still unnoticed by his mother.

"Jesus, Mary, and Saint Joseph!" she exclaimed, jumping up from her position by the oven door and clutching her chest. "Are you trying to give your mother a heart attack? You're early."

"You told me to be here for seven," he replied as he hugged his mother and glanced at the clock: 7:01.

"You feel skinny," she noted as she patted his ribs. "Have you lost weight?"

"Not since I saw you last week at Thanksgiving," Cal said with a roll of his eyes. What was it about Italian women always insisting that everyone was too skinny?

"Calvin Adams, I don't care how old you are. If you roll your eyes at me I'm gonna smack them right out of your head," his mother scolded before she checked her dish in the oven.

"Sorry," Cal said. "Can I help you with anything?"

"Yes. Can you grab some veggies from the fridge and make the salad?"

"Sure." Cal gathered an assortment of crisp vegetables and retrieved a plastic cutting board from one of the stained-wood cabinets. As he began dicing up a juicy tomato, he ruminated on his own relationship failures. No, he couldn't allow himself to think like that—this was Claire's night.

"Hey, Mom," Cal said as he turned his attention toward several thick carrots, which he started to chop. "What do you know about Claire's boyfriend?"

"Well, let's see," she began, while searching through the spice rack for dried oregano. "He's a few years older than her—they met at school. I forget what he's going for, but it's some five-year program, so he'll be finishing up in May."

"Does it sound serious?"

"I think so," his mother said as she leaned against the oven and smiled. "She really likes this guy."

"Oh," Cal replied flatly before he returned his attention to preparing the salad. "That's great."

"So, how about you?" she asked. "Anybody special in your life?"

"Mom, please," he dismissed her, while his face flushed with slight embarrassment.

"What? Is it wrong for me to be asking? I mean, look at you. You're an attractive and successful young man. Any guy would be lucky to be with you."

"No, I'm not seeing anyone. Okay?" Cal retorted, feeling a bit defensive. He always felt awkward and self-conscious whenever his parents pried into his dating life. As his mother was about to add something else to the uncomfortable conversation, the doorbell rang.

"Oh jeez, my lasagna isn't ready yet, and your father's still in the can, and they're here," his mother stammered as she began to hurry around the kitchen. "Are you finished with the salad, hon?"

"Yeah," Cal responded as he handed the bowl over to his mother.

"Todd, hurry up! They're here," she bellowed upstairs before turning back to Cal. "Can you get the door?"

"Sure," he said as he left his frantic mother in the kitchen and entered the foyer. As he approached the door, he began to grow anxious. A family dinner with his sister's boyfriend was a serious occasion, and the gravity of the situation was beginning to dawn on Cal. Would he ever have a serious boyfriend to introduce to his family?

Cal pushed this thought out of his mind as he grasped the handle with a clammy hand and swung the front door open.

Chapter Two

Three and a half years earlier

That fall was Cal's last semester of college, since he would be graduating in early December. He had twelve credits left to complete and most were electives, so it was set to be an easy semester. Due to his light schedule, Cal had ample time to reflect on the past three years. He had engaged in a variety of obligatory collegiate experiences but realized he also missed out on some things.

He had spent much of his time focused on school and marketing himself as a young professional. However, Cal recognized he had not experienced everything he'd thought he would have during these years, which he had been told should be the greatest of his life. He frequently put off going to parties, hanging out with friends, and having fun in other activities around campus so he could concentrate on developing his professional identity. Above all, Cal hadn't dated much during his time at school—besides an awkward first date on occasion—even though he considered himself a hopeless romantic and desired finding a meaningful relationship. Now, with a final semester remaining, he began to regret all he had missed.

Still, there was some time to change things before he graduated, and Cal was ready to make a change—starting with the relationship department. He had recently downloaded several dating apps in the hopes of hitting it off with someone online. Since he had a relaxed schedule, he spent a good deal of his free time utilizing the apps and chatting with various men.

Despite having a light class load that semester, Cal was already struggling with senioritis after his first week of school. Luckily, he had a long weekend since Labor Day was that upcoming Monday. And, even better, he had no classes on Fridays. Cal had been messaging random suitors in the area all week and appeared to have several worthwhile conversations occurring. However, there was someone in particular who he had interacted with on Friday who seemed to stand out among the rest—even before Cal had the chance to get to know him.

He was twenty, a junior at the college down the road from Cal's, and pretty cute—at least from what he could tell based on his profile picture. They had messaged each other via a dating app for several hours, and as the day transitioned into late afternoon, Cal was eager to hang out. He asked him to dinner and this man said he would be free to hang out later that night, after he showered and got ready. An hour and a half later, he sent his phone number and location through the app, and Cal hustled to his car in the nearby lot to pick him up.

The early evening sun seemed to emit a golden glow over the college town, as long shadows were cast across the campus. The late August weather was still very hot and—despite wearing an orange graphic tee, khaki shorts, and flip-flops—Cal was warm, although, that may have been caused by his nerves. Once Cal got into his clunky car, he started the engine and then realized he and his date hadn't exchanged names over the app.

Nevertheless, Cal pulled out his phone to reference the map location he had been sent and began driving into a confusing puzzle of one-way streets in an area of town he wasn't very familiar with. The sent location didn't even have an address—just a geographical reference, so he drove aimlessly down the street and even took a wrong turn. After several minutes of uncertain navigation, Cal parked in front of what he assumed to be the correct apartment and texted his unnamed date to inform him he had arrived. Moments later, without even verifying who Cal was, someone stepped into the car and sank into the passenger seat.

Although Cal had barely gotten a full glance of him, he was overwhelmed by some foreign sensation. His face flushed as his stomach tingled, and Cal became aware of his pounding heart while a wave of heat swept over him from head to toe. Was this what genuine infatuation was? Despite Cal's limited dating experience, he recognized this feeling meant something significant since he had never experienced anything quite like this before.

His date donned a backward snapback—covering his black, medium-length hair—and wore square, diamond-stud earrings, a blue Henley T-shirt with a white patterned design, tan shorts, and black socks that extended past the lining of his sneakers and ran to the midpoint of his calves. He was quite attractive and exuded a cool demeanor.

He didn't exactly resemble his profile picture on the dating app, which was probably an older photo. He appeared less like an incoming, baby-faced college freshman and more like a seasoned twenty-year-old. Regardless, Cal knew right then and there that he wanted him—but not purely in the sexual sense. Cal wanted to know him, Cal wanted to be in a relationship with him, and Cal wanted to always be with him. It was crazy to think that, since he still didn't even know his name.

"Hey, I'm Cal," he introduced himself as the attractive stranger fastened his seat belt.

"I'm Andrew," the young man responded.

They made small talk as Cal drove them over to a part of town consisting of a strip of tiny shops and local restaurants. After Cal parked in a garage, the two began to stroll down Main Street, searching for a place to eat, although Cal had somewhat forgotten to look for a dining location because he could only focus on his conversation with Andrew.

They were both undecided on where to get dinner, but when they reached the end of Main Street, Andrew made Cal pick a location. He chose a small Greek restaurant, which was quiet inside, with one lone patron dining. Besides the sizzle of the grill, the only other noise came from a mounted television in the corner, which was reporting on a comedian's recent death.

"It's sad," Andrew stated, "but it's like the law of thirds." Two other well-known celebrities had died earlier that summer.

Andrew and Cal ordered their food—both got gyros—and sat at a nearby table. Cal was nervous, but did his best to make small talk. His heart was racing while Andrew remained calm, cool, and collected. Cal couldn't help but wonder how Andrew felt: Was he just as nervous?

A short while later, the two finished dinner and walked back to the parking garage. Cal's stomach churned as debated reaching for Andrew's hand during their stroll back to the car, but he was too nervous. Besides, they were out in public and someone might see. Once they reached the parking garage, they settled themselves in Cal's car and an awkward silence fell upon them. Running out of small talk and not sure what to say next, Cal remained quiet as he drove the vehicle out of the garage. Cal's sweaty palms clutched the steering wheel as he drove them back the way they came and soon they made their way across a bridge—one of many in the college town. At the end of the bridge Cal would turn right and take Andrew home...or he could turn left and bring Andrew back to his apartment; they had a decision to make.

"So, do you want me to take you home, or do you want to come over to my place, or...?"

"Yeah, I'll come over," Andrew replied.

Dusk had begun to fall as Cal and Andrew entered his studio apartment, and Cal gave him a brief tour of his pad. Andrew caught a glimpse of the DVD collection adjacent to the television, and they decided to put on a movie. After Andrew had perused the titles for a few minutes, he selected an older horror movie. Cal set up the film and then settled himself next to Andrew on the tiny twin bed. He was anxious and nervous and paid more attention to Andrew's movements out of the corner of his eye than to the movie. Gradually, their hands edged closer to one another until Andrew grasped Cal's clammy palm.

"Do you want to lie down?" Andrew suggested after several minutes of holding hands and stroking each other's arms.

"Yeah, sure," Cal replied.

"I like being little spoon," he stated as he lay his head on a pillow.

"Cool. I like being big spoon," Cal responded before he wrapped his arms around Andrew.

Although he had met Andrew a couple of hours ago, lying with him seemed intimate, as Cal hoped it would. And while they may have just been "acquaintances" at that moment, they soon moved past the awkward small talk and began to open up a bit.

"So, are you out?" he asked after conversing for a bit.

"Yeah," Cal said. "How about you?"

"No, but I'm bi, so I don't see coming out as a big issue," Andrew explained. "How about you?"

"I'm gay," he informed him.

"So when we were talking on the app, you said you're not into hookups. Are you a virgin?"

"Yeah."

"Oh, okay."

"Like, I'm not saying I'm waiting for marriage, but I want to wait until I'm in a serious relationship with someone."

"Aw, that's cool. That's what I did," Andrew said. "I was in a relationship with a guy for a while."

"Oh, cool," Cal replied. "Um, so...were you a top or a bottom?"

"Well," he responded with a slight chuckle, "I kind of have a big dick, so I was a bottom. Cause...you know...not everyone can take all of it."

They continued talking while watching the movie, but soon talking turned into kissing—passionate kissing. Mouths wide open, hands groping one another, they took their shirts off. Things were moving a little faster than Cal was used to, but it seemed right. Andrew's hand drifted from Cal's shoulder to his hips, gripping the waist of his shorts and then casually slipping over his crotch. Cal grabbed his wrist and pulled Andrew's hand out of his shorts.

Chapter Three

Cal grasped the doorknob with a clammy hand and pulled it open.

"Oh shit," Cal muttered unintentionally. His stomach sank and his face flushed as he gaped in disbelief at the ghost in front of him.

Standing there on the porch step was his sister, Claire. She was petite in stature—standing at just over five feet in height with the assistance of a stylish pair of brown high-heeled boots—with dark hair that fell past her slim shoulders and gentle gray eyes almost identical to Cal's. Her face—which bore minimal makeup—was naturally attractive and resembled that of their mother's. And standing by Claire's side was her boyfriend, Andrew.

Claire had released a squeal of delight as she pursed her glossy plump lips at the same time, which drowned out his cuss. She flung her arms around Cal and hugged him, since she had not seen him in months. Behind her back, Andrew stared with his brown eyes wide in shock. Clearly, he had not expected Cal to reappear in his life either. However, as Claire released Cal from her warm embrace, Andrew masked his surprise.

"Cal, I want you to meet my *boyfriend*," Claire announced with a flirtatious smile toward Andrew. The word *boyfriend* struck Cal like a slap to the face. "This is Andrew Hall."

"Hi, nice to meet you," Andrew said and extended his hand. He acted convincing as if it were the first time the two men had met each other. Cal shook his hand weakly and stared in blank shock at his former flame.

"Hi," Cal replied.

"Aren't you gonna tell him your name?" Claire inquired with a puzzled glance at her brother, sensing something was off.

"I'm pretty sure he already knows who I am," Cal blurted out with a hint of distaste, which slipped out before he realized what he had said. Now, with Andrew—his little sister's *boyfriend*—standing on his parents' porch, he couldn't control his words. The lingering heartache he had dealt with over the years had transformed to...anger?

"What?" Claire asked; Andrew seemed nervous.

"Uh—I mean, I'm pretty sure he already knows who I am," Cal replied in a faked, enthusiastic tone as he tried to recover. "You just said my name when you introduced him, duh."

Cal's already flushed face grew even redder as he stammered. It was bad enough that Claire brought home his secret ex, but now he was making an idiot of himself in front of Andrew. Cal's embarrassment increased when he realized he was still shaking Andrew's hand.

"I'm Cal," he said and released Andrew's hand. The trio glanced at one another for a moment as they stood at the door, under the flurrying night sky.

"Um..." Claire began as she shivered in the crisp December air.

"Oh yeah. Come in. Come in," Cal said. "Uh, I'm gonna start drinking—I mean, does anyone need...want a drink? No? Okay, I'm just gonna run...I mean, I gotta grab something upstairs—"

His mother had swooped in to greet Claire's boyfriend, which allowed Cal to escape up the stairs. As he reached the hallway on the upper level, Cal strode past his father, who had finally exited the bathroom.

"Everything all right, son?"

"Oh yeah," Cal lied. "I just need to...yeah."

He hurried into his childhood bedroom, which had recently been turned into the guest room, and shut the door. His parents had repainted the walls a soft cream shade, which had a matching colored bedspread and window curtains. Their rationale was that the neutral colors would provide a relaxing and comfortable environment for their guests. However, Cal was anything but relaxed as he retrieved his phone from his pocket.

"Hello?" Sophie answered on the third ring.

"It's me," he replied.

"What's up? Aren't you supposed to be having that family dinner tonight?"

"Yeah, it's happening right now. Claire's *boyfriend* just got here."

"Ooh, is he cute?" Sophie wondered playfully.

"It's Andrew."

"Andrew?" she repeated, unsure of what Cal had meant. "Wait, *Andrew*? No, you don't mean—"

"Fuckface? Yep, it's him," he stated.

"Are you sure?"

"Well, I can't be sure. I didn't get a good look at his dick yet," Cal snapped. "Of course I'm sure!"

"Okay, okay. Relax," Sophie replied.

"Sorry, it's just...ugh, what do I do?"

"Did he recognize you?"

"Oh yeah, he seemed just as shocked as I was."

"Oh shit" was all Sophie was able to say. She remembered how distraught Cal had been over the Andrew situation three and a half years ago. And while she had never had a turbulent relationship as he apparently did, she could appreciate the resulting heartache from it. She knew feelings like that did not just go away—even three and a half years later. "Well, what happened?"

"I opened the door, made an idiot out of myself, and then ran upstairs to my old room to call you."

"Wait, they just got there and you ran off?" Sophie asked. "You need to go back downstairs."

"I know. It's just, I still... It's just hard to face him," Cal muttered. "After everything that happened, you know?"

"Yeah, I know," she replied in a tone of genuine sympathy for her friend. "Did he say anything to you?"

"No, he acted like it was the first time we met."

"And you never told your parents or Claire about him?"

"You're the only one who knows. I never told them about *him*," Cal admitted. If he had told his parents about Andrew years ago, then maybe they would've encouraged him to stay in his old college town instead of accepting his first job and moving out of state. Maybe then he would be the one bringing Andrew home to meet his family instead of Claire. But, sad to say, that hadn't happened and now he had to deal with the consequences. "What do I do?"

"Well first, you need to go back downstairs," Sophie reasoned. "Your family will know something's up if you're in your room all night."

"Ugh, do I have to?" he grumbled.

"Yes, you do," Sophie said in a firm tone. "I know this situation sucks, but maybe it's for the best. Maybe this is the closure you need."

"Yeah, I guess you're right," Cal sighed.

"You'll be all right. Show him what he missed out on," Sophie advised him. Still, she could sense Cal's solemnness through the phone. "And call me if you need anything."

"Oh, I'm sure I will. Thanks, Sophie," Cal replied. After he hung up, he heaved a deep sigh and rubbed his weary eyes. The man who had caused him so much pain—unbeknownst to his family—was in his parents' house. But now, he wasn't just Cal's crush and ex; he was Claire's *boyfriend*. He was Claire's *serious boyfriend*. Cal could only imagine how his parents were gawking over Andrew downstairs, unaware that he had ever broken their son's heart.

Seriously, who else would this happen to? Cal mused before he left the safety of his parents' guest room and traipsed downstairs to face his former flame, with his family as an audience. When he arrived downstairs, Andrew, Claire, and their father were all seated at the dining room table while his mother extracted the steaming lasagna from the toasty oven.

"Honey, are you all right? You seem flustered," Mrs. Adams observed.

"Yeah, I'm fine," Cal replied, attempting to sound as composed as possible. "I just felt a headache coming on."

"Oh, do you need something? I've got some ibuprofen in the medicine cabinet," she offered as she began to grab silverware from a nearby drawer.

"I'm gonna need something stronger than that," he mumbled under his breath.

"What?"

"I said, 'No thanks.' I'm good."

"Okay, well dinner is just about ready," his mother informed him. "Why don't you go sit at the table."

"Um, is there anything you need help with?" Cal asked, desperate to buy himself a few additional minutes before having to face Andrew at the dinner table.

"Nope, I think I'm all good here."

"You sure?"

"Awe, you're sweet, honey. But everything's pretty much ready to go out," she said. At his mother's insistence, Cal trudged out of the kitchen and reluctantly entered the dining room. He took up a strategic position next to his father, who was seated at the head of the table. Claire sat across from Cal, with Andrew next to her. The couple smiled and laughed among themselves as Cal's stomach churned and his heart sank.

"Hey, bud. Want some wine?" Mr. Adams inquired, raising a large bottle of Cabernet Sauvignon.

"Hell, yes," Cal sighed and held out his glass. His father cast him a suspicious expression. "I mean, yes, please."

"All right, I hope you're hungry, Andrew. I made tons of food," Mrs. Adams stated as she came into the dining room with the lasagna, which she placed upon the glass tabletop among numerous side dishes.

"Jeez, Mom. How many people are you planning to feed?" Claire teased.

"I know, I know. I always make too much food," she admitted as she sat at the other end of the table. "I can't help it. I'm Italian."

"Everything looks great, Mrs. Adams," Andrew complimented.

Kiss ass, Cal thought.

"Well, thank you, sweetie," she said with a warm smile before she raised her wine glass. "Before we start eating, I would like to say thank you for joining us for dinner, Andrew. We've heard so many great things from Claire, but I'm glad we finally get to meet you in person. *Salute!*"

"*Salute!*" those around the table chimed in before they clinked their glasses.

"Cheers," Cal grumbled without raising his drink. Instead, he brought it to his lips and emptied the glass. He placed the empty cup upon the table—harder than he had intended—and began to pour himself some more wine.

"Cal," his mother hissed.

"Sorry, I did a quick workout before I left work. I'm a little dehydrated," he lied as he sipped his wine.

"How is the gym, Cal?" Claire inquired, trying to smooth over the awkwardness.

"It's good. Same old, same old."

"Oh, do you work at a gym?" Andrew asked.

"Yep, I manage it," he responded curtly.

"Yeah, Cal manages a local gym about half an hour or so from here," Claire explained to Andrew. "He's been there, what, two and a half years now?"

"Yep, two and a half years now. Yep," Cal answered as he took another sip of Cabernet Sauvignon.

"Do you live around here then?" Andrew wondered.

"I do. I live by my gym, so about half an hour away," he replied and paused. "Actually, it's a funny story. I went to school about a mile or so away from your college. Well, yours and Claire's. Now that I think about it, it's a pretty small college town. I'm surprised we never bumped each other—bumped *into* each other before.

"Anyway, I graduated about three years ago and moved out of state for a job. But I was going through some shit—"

"No language at the table, please," his mother interjected.

"I'm sorry, *stuff*. I was going through some stuff and had a hard time with the move, so I wound up quitting. Then, I came back this way and became a gym manager," Cal finished. "Innit funny how life turns out?"

"Uh, well it's lucky you're doing something related to your degree," Andrew replied, his face now flushing. Was he nervous? "I mean, I'm assuming you went to school for business management, since you're managing a gym. A lot of grads are having trouble finding jobs in their field."

"Speaking of which, you're still in school, right?" Mr. Adams asked.

"Yeah, I'm in a five-year program so I'll be graduating in May," he informed them.

"You know, Cal and I were just talking about this before you got here," Mrs. Adams began. Cal groaned under his breath as his face flushed in embarrassment once again. "What are you majoring in?"

"Forensic science," Andrew replied.

"And he's minoring in Spanish and anthropology," Claire added.

"Oh wow, that's impressive!" Cal said, sounding a little too enthusiastic, but no one at the table seemed to pick up on his fake tone.

"It really is," his mother agreed. "What do you want to do with that after you graduate?"

"I'm hoping to work in a forensics lab," Andrew explained. "I've been looking into some companies near my school."

"Andrew just finished up an internship with our school's cadaver lab," Claire informed the table.

"Oh, that's great," their mother said. "What did you do?"

"Mostly grunt work, but it was a great opportunity, and I learned a lot," Andrew said. "I had to remove various organs from the cadavers and perform tests on them to determine their different pathologies."

"How did you like that?" Mr. Adams inquired.

"I loved it," Andrew replied with a smile.

Yeah, I'm sure you loved ripping hearts out of bodies, Cal thought bitterly as he took a large gulp of his wine.

Perhaps it was the two glasses of wine Cal consumed within ten minutes on an empty stomach or maybe it was the emotional turmoil he was experiencing. Regardless, the events and conversation over dinner that evening blurred together. Andrew was well received by his parents, who lauded his academic accomplishments and career pursuits. Claire, who had appeared tense upon their arrival, seemed at ease as she conversed and beamed at her boyfriend. Meanwhile, Cal ate his dinner in silence while holding back his scoffs and avoiding eye contact with Andrew.

An hour and a half later, the dinner came to a close as Andrew and the Adamses sat around the table with mugs of coffee. Cal was quite full, having kept his mouth full of food to avoid speaking during the meal. The slight state of drunkenness he may have felt during the meal had now dissipated thanks to the large dinner and the caffeine of his black coffee, which had accompanied dessert.

The company continued to converse as they picked at the scrumptious homemade apple crisp that Mrs. Adams had prepared. Once Mr. Adams had finished his coffee, he began to clear the empty dessert plates, and Mrs. Adams rose from her own seat to assist her husband. Cal refused to be left alone with his former flame and his sister and took this opportunity to head home to his apartment.

"Hun, I don't think it's a good idea for you to go home," his mother called from the kitchen. She was gazing out the window over the sink as she rinsed off a serving platter while Mr. Adams stood beside her and loaded plates into the dishwasher.

"Why?" Cal asked as he retrieved his coat from the hall closet.

"The roads are pretty bad," she explained as she continued to stare out the window. "Come here. Look."

At her request, Cal traipsed over to his mother and gazed out the window. The swirling snow flurries from earlier had transformed into a heavy snowfall during dinner, and the unplowed roads were coated with at least six inches of the cruel, frigid white powder.

"Oh, I don't think they're that bad," Cal lied since he was eager to leave Andrew behind and get back to his apartment. Cal's eyes diverted from the winter storm over to his beat-up car. It was a solid silhouette of white, completely engulfed by the thick snow.

"Cal, I don't think you should drive," Mrs. Adams said, her voice full of concern.

"It's just a little dusting," he insisted, unwilling to be stuck in the house another minute.

"There's a bad pileup on the main road," Mr. Adams announced from the family room, where he was now standing in front of the television and watching the local news. "They're shutting it down."

"Well, that's what back roads are for," Cal shrugged.

"The back roads are going to be worse," his mother stated.

"Mom, my car is solid. It can hold its own in the snow."

"Cal, you're staying here," she insisted.

"I don't have any clothes or anything," he countered.

"That's okay, you can borrow some of your father's things."

"But—"

"I'll go grab them now," his mother cut him off and left the kitchen at a swift clip, having the final say in the matter.

Cal groaned. Out of all the men at his sister's college, why did Claire have to date *him*? What were the odds? And to make matters worse, Cal was snowed in his parents' house with his ex and unsuspecting family. How could this have happened? Was this some sort of sick joke?

Unwilling to converse with his family and Andrew, Cal swiped a half-empty bottle of whiskey from his parents' liquor cabinet and hustled upstairs to the guest room. He shut the door behind him and spied a pile of clothes his mother had set out for him at the foot of the bed. Though he could use Sophie's encouraging spirit right now, Cal was much too emotionally drained to talk about Andrew any further.

"Well, fuck," was all Cal was able to mutter as he replayed the night's events in his head.

Exhausted—both physically and mentally—and wanting temporary relief to ease his heartache, Cal opened the bottle of whiskey and took a long swig of the strong liquor. It burned a bit as it trickled down his throat with a warming sensation. Then, he changed into a pair of his father's red flannel lounge pants and a faded gray tee—both of which were at least two sizes too big on him—before collapsing onto the bed. He continued to drink from the bottle, growing dizzier and number with each sip until soon his memories of Andrew were just a blur. Within half an hour, the drowsing effect of the whiskey had consumed Cal, and he fell asleep.

Chapter Four

Three and a half years earlier

A random heat wave swept through the college town during the first week of October, with temperatures reaching the midseventies. The owners of Cal's apartment building were unprepared for the mild weather of early October and had shut the air-conditioning off the week prior, leaving the units sweltering.

One afternoon, as Cal was cooling off in a tank top and basketball shorts, he received a text message. Unrelated to the heat, Cal began sweating as he saw who it was—Andrew.

Hey man it's been a while. How's it going?

Cal began to type in an attempt to sound nonchalant despite his heart skipping erratically and his hands shaking.

Ha ha yeah. And it's going. Just been busy with school hbu?

Andrew continued to text Cal, as if the silence from the past several weeks had never occurred. Why had he waited almost a month to reply? Their first date seemed to have gone well, and Andrew's touch had communicated an intimate attraction to Cal; wasn't that enough? Over the past few weeks of silence, Cal had wanted to text him, but feared Andrew's withdrawal was a sign of lost interest. Still, he couldn't quite accept that and had hoped that Andrew would come back around. He had to admit that Andrew's timing was a bit peculiar, and perhaps even a bit shady, but Cal wanted to give him the benefit of the doubt. Maybe Andrew had been equally as nervous and was waiting for Cal to text him. Whatever the reason may be, the important thing was Andrew was texting him again.

The two messaged each other over the next several days. Cal began to notice that Andrew had a tendency to stop replying mid-conversation and wouldn't text him back until a day or two later. Was he playing games with Cal or was he unaware of how much Cal looked forward to hearing from him?

After a week and a half of sporadic messaging, Cal had had enough. If Andrew still wanted him, then great, and if he didn't...well fine. But texting back and forth without making any definite plans to meet was frustrating for Cal. One Thursday evening as he was getting ready for bed, Cal attempted to gain control of the situation:

We should hang out again.

Cal held his breath as the text message was sent; it was the moment of truth.

Yeah I'd like that. Andrew responded several minutes later.

Cool when are you free?

How about tomorrow nite?

Cal's face flushed and his stomach churned anxiously as he read Andrew's message.

Yeah sounds good

He and Andrew made arrangements to watch movies at Cal's apartment. Andrew had to assist at a volunteer event on behalf of a student organization that night, so he asked Cal to pick him up afterward around nine.

Cal parked his car across from Andrew's apartment and his heart raced in eager anticipation. His phone cast a soft glow through the darkness of that October evening as he texted Andrew to inform him he had arrived. Cal experienced an odd sense of déjà vu while he waited; had it actually been over a month since he was last there?

After a few minutes, Andrew emerged from one of the apartments, and Cal experienced that familiar sense of attraction sweep through his entire being just as strong as it had been the first time they met. Andrew climbed into the car, and they drove over to Cal's place.

Once they were inside, he was able to get a good look at Andrew in the light. Cal couldn't believe he was in the company of this man once again, who was just as handsome as Cal had remembered.

"I love your beard," Andrew complimented. "It seems a lot thicker now."

Yeah, isn't it funny what can change in a month? Cal mused. Nevertheless, he dismissed his annoyance with Andrew's month-long silence because he was there.

The two picked up where they left off as they conversed and laughed with each other until they decided to pick out a movie to watch. They made themselves comfortable on the bed as Andrew eased himself into Cal's arms. Cal's heart raced as their two bodies reconnected with each other, and he felt the touch which he had craved since the night they met in August.

After a short while, Cal and Andrew shifted their attention from the movie to each other. A gentle breeze sailed through an open window in the apartment as they gazed with longing into each other's eyes; there was no denying the attraction. Passion took over as Cal and Andrew locked lips.

Andrew climbed on top of Cal and combed his fingers through his soft chest hair. The two continued kissing as Cal's hands drifted from Andrew's broad shoulders, sliding down his smooth back until they groped his thick buttocks. In response to his touch, he gave Cal's lip a playful nibble. Then Andrew placed his lips on his neck and kissed him tenderly as Cal released a soft groan.

The unseasonably warm October night seemed to grow hotter as Cal and Andrew reignited their romance. The two men soon began perspiring and stripped down to their underwear, both in an effort to stay cool and a desire for further intimacy.

They continued to grope and kiss each other while rolling around in the bed until Andrew lay flat on his back, placing his calves on Cal's slender shoulders as he knelt above him.

"What are you doing?" Cal asked and chuckled.

"If we were gonna have sex, this would be the usual position," Andrew explained. He placed his hands around Cal's waist and pulled him closer, so his groin was pressed against Andrew.

"Oh yeah?" Cal inquired. Though he was unsure of how to respond without sounding foolish, his body reacted with instinct to Andrew's words and he grew increasingly hard.

"But in porn," Andrew began with a laugh as he and Cal broke apart. He positioned Cal at the edge of the bed and then sat on his lap, face-to-face, before leaning back. "I've also seen it done like *this*."

After Andrew's demonstrations of various sex positions, the two resumed kissing, and they held each other close. Their bodies were damp with perspiration, and Cal could feel a few stray beads of sweat drip down his chest. Andrew slipped his thumb under the elastic trim of Cal's underwear.

"Is this okay?" he asked while he ran his thumb along Cal's waistline.

"Yeah," he breathed. Andrew slid his hand farther down and began to stroke Cal's erect penis. In response, Cal ran his hand over Andrew's groin, which was also hard. He grasped Andrew's erection and began stroking it.

Andrew groaned and slid Cal's underwear down to his ankles. Peering into each other's eyes, they lay on their sides stroking each other and pleasure tingled through their warm bodies. Suddenly, Cal went limp. Andrew's touch had been more than satisfying, but it was too much too soon.

"I'm sorry, I don't think I'm ready for this," Cal admitted, his face turning red with blush, and he pulled his underwear up to cover himself.

"Nah, it's cool," Andrew replied as he tucked his own still-erect penis back into his underwear.

The two men lay side-by-side on their backs—still shirtless and pantless—as they caught their breath. Then, Cal leaned over and placed his lips upon Andrew's. They continued to make out for a while longer until Andrew decided it was time to leave, and Cal drove him home. He was mortified that he had become flaccid in front of Andrew. Cal liked him a lot, but he wasn't prepared to go that far.

Despite Cal's embarrassment over the situation, Andrew didn't seem to mind. The two continued to text more than they had in the past and even made plans for the following week. To get in the Halloween spirit, they decided to go to a haunted house and even held hands the entire time—which seemed promising since Andrew claimed he was not into public displays of affection. Per usual, the night ended at Cal's apartment where they cuddled on Cal's bed since Andrew was exhausted.

"I could just lie here forever," Andrew muttered, and he gave Cal a peck on the lips.

It all seemed too good to be true. Over a month ago, Cal had been crushed by Andrew's silence. But now, here they were on his bed; who would've ever thought? Andrew's words made Cal's heart skip a beat and, for a moment, he believed maybe he and Andrew could actually be together. *I could just lie here forever.*

It was a nice sentiment, but unfortunately they were empty words. A week and a half later, Cal had to leave the state to interview for a business management position with a prestigious company. He had interned with the organization over the two previous summers, so the interview was a formality.

As an intern, Cal was excited at the prospect of working for the business and becoming a permanent part of the team. But now, as he was halfway through his final college semester and his romance with Andrew appeared to be back on track, he didn't know what he wanted after graduation. However, Cal made the mistake of telling Andrew about the interview, which seemed to have gone well.

He seemed somewhat quiet the next couple of days. Then, Cal awoke one morning to a text Andrew had sent him around midnight.

Hey so I've been lying in bed thinking about you.

I just wanted to let you know that if it seems like I'm backing off, you didn't do anything wrong. I like you but you mite be leaving the state after you graduate and I don't want to get too attached.

As soon as Cal finished reading the message, he responded. He tried to tell Andrew that nothing was certain yet. Cal hadn't been offered the job—though he feared he would—and graduation was still two months away; a lot could happen in that time.

Andrew agreed. However, he never responded when Cal suggested they hang out later that week. Once again, a familiar silence smothered what Cal had hoped to be a budding romance. And this time, it seemed permanent.

Chapter Five

The morning after the disastrous family dinner, Cal awoke groggily with a dull headache. As he rubbed his dry eyes he recalled a most peculiar dream, which still haunted him as he roused himself. A familiar pair of brown eyes had crept back into his life, and their owner was intent on breaking Cal's heart once again. In his dream, the seductive heartbreaker infiltrated the foundation Cal had rebuilt over the past few years by romancing Claire and winning over his parents. Like a disease, the handsome menace had attacked Cal from within until his heart, body, and sanity crumbled from despair.

Cal grew alert as he heard the squeak of the shower knob turning in the bathroom adjacent to his room. He had been unaware of the sound of running water, but now that the faucet was off, the resulting silence was deafening. Still disoriented from last night's whiskey, Cal glanced around and realized he was not in his apartment, but the guest room of his parents' house, and the events of the past twenty-four hours raced through his mind, adding to his pain. Dinner, the snowstorm, *Andrew*. It had not just been a peculiar dream; Cal was trapped in a nightmare.

Soft voices murmured in the kitchen below as the bitter aroma of coffee wafted upstairs. Cal's slight headache began to throb as he sat up in bed, and his stomach lurched, although he was not sure if that was caused by his emotional distress or mild hangover. After several minutes of debating, Cal determined he was more hungry than nauseous and decided to go downstairs to grab a cup of coffee and a light breakfast.

He eased himself out of bed and rubbed his forehead, hoping to comfort his headache. He readjusted the elastic waistband of the loose-fitting lounge pants—which had been sagging below his waist—and then exited the guestroom. He could make out the voices of Claire and their parents as he stepped into the upstairs hallway. Then the bathroom door opened and Andrew stood in front of Cal.

His skin was shiny and damp, and only a soft, tan towel was wrapped around his waist. The wind was knocked out of Cal as he gazed upon his former lover's semi-nude body. When was the last time he had seen this much of Andrew? The night they made love?

Cal had been so shocked by Andrew's arrival the night prior that he had not taken the time to observe the changes in his ex. Andrew's dark hair—now damp and clinging to his forehead—had not changed. His face, once smooth and clean-shaven, now sported a light patch of facial hair on his chin and upper lip. Still, he maintained the same youthful and carefree complexion as before. His once hairless body now had a small tuft of chest hair, and his torso appeared to be a bit softer than it had been three years ago. Although his appearance had changed, the resemblance to his former self was obvious. And there was no denying Cal's longing for him.

"Uh, hey," Andrew said and smiled weakly, unsure of what to say now that he and Cal were alone together for the first time in years.

Cal rolled his eyes and began to walk past Andrew.

"Cal, wait a minute," Andrew pleaded. "I want to talk to you."

"Oh, now you want to talk?" Cal hissed. "Three and a half fucking years later, and you want to talk now?"

"I get it—"

"Do you?" Cal interrupted. "Do you know how it feels to have spent four months—my last semester of college—wondering if I'd ever see you again, and making myself available to you whenever you were interested and then not hear anything from you after?"

"I know, it wasn't fair for me—"

"No, it *wasn't* fair. At all," he snapped. "Do you know that for years I've wondered what we were? If you actually ever liked me or if I was just a convenience for you."

"You're right, it was really shitty of me—"

"And then, you came to my apartment and said we'd talk about *us* the next day. We had sex and then you left. Do you know what that felt like? Waking up the next morning and you were gone?"

"Cal, I'm sorry. I'm so sorry," Andrew said with a solemn expression, which was similar to the one he wore on the night when he had arrived without notice at Cal's apartment. "I don't know what I can say. I was young. I was scared."

"You were scared!" Cal retorted. "You know, all I'm hearing is 'Me, me, me, me, me.' *You* were young; *you* were scared; *you* didn't want to get too attached. What about me, Andrew? *I* was young. *I* was scared too. For Christ's sake, I was the one moving out of state while wondering—"

"Exactly, *you* were moving!" Andrew countered. His usual carefree demeanor had been broken. "You were gonna be leaving. So can you really blame me?"

"Yeah, I was leaving," Cal acknowledged with his voice trembling ever so slightly in a mixture of anger and anguish. "But if you had given me a reason—even if you had just said *something*—I would've stayed."

Andrew opened his mouth, as if he wanted to say something, but instead sighed deeply and was at a loss for words.

"But instead, you kept your distance and only came around when you wanted to," Cal spat. He was surprised by how strong his tone of voice was, despite feeling like an emotional wreck. "What? Did you just hit me up when you were bored and horny?"

"No! Cal, come on. I...I don't know what to say," Andrew admitted with a tinge of regret. "I don't know what I can say to fix this."

"There's nothing you can say to fix this," he retorted.

"Cal, you were never just a convenience."

It had taken three and a half years, but Cal was finally receiving answers to the questions he had. Andrew had said exactly what he had hoped to hear for so long: he was never just a convenience. However, Andrew's words meant nothing to Cal now, much to his surprise. His words provided no sense of relief or closure. Standing in front of Andrew left Cal feeling just as heartbroken as when he had woken up in bed alone on the day of his graduation.

"Even if I wasn't, I still made it easy for you to walk out on. You were able to go on with your life, without any thoughts of me. I'm the one who still has feelings for you, who can't move on after all these years," Cal blurted out as his body grew rigid from embarrassment. He could not believe he had let that slip.

"You still have feelings for me?" Andrew inquired in a soft voice. Cal knew he had trapped himself in his confession. If he denied his statement, then he would be caught in a lie. But if he confirmed his feelings, then he would sound pathetic. Whatever he replied, he couldn't win.

"I know. How fucked up is that?" Cal scoffed and rolled his eyes at his own foolishness.

"I've always thought about you," Andrew admitted. "A lot."

"Well, that doesn't help me any," Cal dismissed. His family continued chattering downstairs over breakfast, unaware of the awkward reconciliation of former lovers above them. "You're with my sister now."

"I swear, I had no idea she was your sister," Andrew stated, raising his hands in defense.

"I figured," Cal replied.

"And...I mean...she didn't say anything about—"

"I never told them."

"What do you mean?"

"I never told Claire or my parents about...about *us*."

"Oh, okay," Andrew replied. An uncomfortable silence settled between the two men, who avoided eye contact with each other. Cal shifted his attention from Andrew's eyes to his chest where he noticed a few stray droplets of water dripping from his half-naked body, which had now dried somewhat.

"Yeah, well..." Cal mumbled as he began to walk away down the hall.

"Wait," he said as Cal reached the top of the staircase.

"Yeah?" he replied, glancing back at Andrew over his shoulder.

"I know you never told your family," he began, "but, um...can we keep it that way?"

"What?" Cal asked—though he knew what Andrew had meant—and turned around to face him.

"Can we keep *us* to ourselves?" Andrew asked. "I don't want Claire to know."

"Wow, you haven't changed at all," Cal chuckled in disbelief. "You're still only concerned about yourself."

"Come on, Cal. This is a weird situation we're in."

"Andrew, are you done in the shower?" Claire called before she appeared at the foot of the stairs. "Oh, Cal, you're finally up."

"Yeah, I was exhausted," he stated.

"I hope I'm not interrupting anything," she said as she glanced between the two men with a bemused expression on her face.

Andrew shot Cal a nervous expression, and his eyes begged for silence.

"No," Cal replied after a moment's hesitation, "you're not interrupting anything."

"We were just talking," Andrew added.

"About growing a pair," Cal snickered under his breath.

"All right, well glad you guys are getting to know each other," Claire said, without having heard Cal. "We made breakfast, so come down and have something to eat."

"We'll be right there," Cal replied. Once Claire was out of earshot, he turned back toward Andrew. "Don't worry, I'm not going to say anything."

"Thank you," Andrew sighed, appearing relieved.

"But I'm not doing this for you," he replied in a cool tone as he walked away. Cal strode downstairs to join his family for breakfast, leaving Andrew behind in the hallway.

Cal greeted his parents as he entered the toasty kitchen and helped himself to a warmed, plain bagel, absent of any sort of butter or spread, which was all his stomach could handle. As Cal chowed down on his breakfast, he gazed out the window. The snowstorm had continued throughout the night and covered his hometown in a cozy blanket of cool white powder. The roads appeared to have been plowed earlier that morning, however they were still slick and covered with fresh snow as relentless flurries fell from the cloudy sky. Cal wouldn't be returning to his apartment anytime soon.

As he was finishing his bagel, Andrew entered the kitchen and the two avoided eye contact with each other as he was welcomed by the Adamses. Cal scarfed down the rest of his bagel and then hurried upstairs to the guest room, eager to spend as little time as possible around his ex. He wanted to lay low until the roads improved so he could escape from the awkwardness enveloping his parents' home. However, he knew he could not hide out in the guest room until the winter storm broke, so he decided he would shower.

He welcomed the therapeutic warmth of the hot water as it rained from the showerhead and trickled down his chilled flesh. The heat provided a sense of comfort and ease despite Cal's troubling circumstances. After several minutes, steam began to accumulate in the bathroom and with it came a familiar scent, which stung his nostrils—*Andrew*. He realized Andrew had left his shampoo and body wash in the shower. For a moment, standing under the steamy water and smelling his ex's scent, Cal felt as if he was being embraced by Andrew once more.

His reverie was broken as a sudden fit of laughter resounded from downstairs. No doubt Andrew had probably said something humorous, much to his family's delight. Cal was somewhat frustrated that they were fawning over his former flame, though he knew he was being irrational. He had kept silent about Andrew for years, so how could he blame his parents for not recognizing his displeasure? And he certainly could understand why Claire had fallen for her boyfriend. As average as Andrew may have been, something about his touch and demeanor proved to be intoxicating.

Once he finished washing himself, Cal got out of the shower and changed into his father's clothes—baggy worn jeans and a shapeless concert tee from the late eighties. Cal sighed as he peered into the bathroom mirror and critiqued his appearance. He resembled his former teenaged self, wearing loose-fitting clothes and feeling insecure. The only thing worse than facing Andrew was to face Andrew like that. Despite his embarrassment, Cal forced himself to rejoin his family downstairs.

Prior to the winter storm, Mr. and Mrs. Adams had planned on getting their Christmas tree from the local tree farm. However, since they were now snowed in, Mrs. Adams decided to clean and put out her holiday décor instead, and she recruited the rest of the family—and Andrew—to assist with decorating.

The snow outside continued to fall as the company adorned the cozy home with various Christmas trinkets, and they took a brief break for lunch. Cal and Andrew avoided each other whenever possible but cast awkward glances on occasion. As the afternoon progressed, Cal slipped into the hallway to assist his mother with stringing garland on the banister of the stairs.

"So...what do you think of Andrew?" his mother asked eventually, out of earshot of the others.

"What do *you* think of Andrew?" Cal questioned without removing his attention from a strand of lights, which he was in the process of wrapping around the garland.

"I like him a lot," she responded. "He seems like a great guy."

"Yeah, he seems fine."

"That sounded sincere," his mother stated and chuckled a little. "You don't like him?"

"No, Mom. I do like him," Cal said; he wasn't lying. "Like I said, he seems fine."

"Then what's with the tone?"

"I just don't feel well, that's all. I think I'm coming down with something."

"Oh, do you still have a headache?" she asked.

"Yeah."

"The medicine didn't help? It didn't get any better?"

"Nope, the headache feels *a lot* worse," Cal replied.

"Well, hopefully it's just the weather. The snow is supposed to let up tonight."

Great, guess I'm gonna be stuck here another night, Cal thought.

Despite the forecast, the snow continued to fall into the early evening and showed no signs of letting up anytime soon. Cal was forced to stay overnight at his parents' house once again, much to his dismay. He turned in for the night early, desperate to escape from Andrew and his unsuspecting family. However, Cal struggled to fall asleep as he replayed his brief fling with Andrew over and over in his head. The endless thoughts of his ex resulted in a cruel dream of the two of them getting back together, feeling young, naïve, and in love. However, in the chill of the next morning, he was reminded that it was not so. The snow had finally eased up sometime during the night. However, the roads were still messy, so Mr. and Mrs. Adams convinced Cal to stay until the plows were able to clear up the streets. Cal was emotionally exhausted and had no energy left to be in the presence of Andrew, so he grabbed a book from the study and retreated back to the guest room.

Around five, his parents determined the roads were suitable to drive on. Cal grabbed what little belongings he had brought with him—unaware on Friday night that he would be trapped with his ex all weekend—and hurried to leave, much to his parents' disappointment.

"Honey, can't you stay for dinner?" his mother inquired as Cal grabbed his coat from the hall closet.

"I really can't, Mom," Cal replied and gave her a quick hug. "I've got a lot of stuff to get done before tomorrow."

"All right," she sighed.

"Well, we'll see you soon," Claire said as she gave her brother a warm hug goodbye.

"You will?" Cal asked with a puzzled expression.

"Christmas," Claire replied with a giggle.

"Oh, that's right."

"Andrew's going to spend Christmas with us too," she informed him.

"They're going to be with us the whole week before Christmas," their mother added cheerfully while Cal gave his father a handshake and a pat on the shoulder. "Since they have a couple weeks off for winter break, they thought it would be nice to stay here and spend some time with the family."

"What?" Cal said.

"Ow!" his father exclaimed and then laughed. "That's some handshake you've got there, son. Is that how you lock potential clients into a gym membership?"

"Sorry, Dad," Cal apologized as he released his father's hand. "Well, that's...great. Andrew's going to be here. That will be fun. That will be *fun*."

"Cal, you should try to take some time off that week and come over," his mother suggested.

"I wish I could, but this is my busy season," he reasoned. "A lot of people want to start their New Year's resolutions early."

"Oh, okay," she replied, sounding discouraged.

"Well, I'll see you guys soon though," Cal said as he began to walk out the door, feeling a bit guilty for his mother's disappointment.

"Wait, I think Andrew's upstairs using the bathroom," Claire said. "Don't you want to say goodbye?"

"You know, I really don't—can't," Cal stammered as he walked to his car. "I'm in a big rush, but I'll see him at Christmas. It will be fun! See ya!"

Cal started his car and allowed the engine to warm up while he brushed the snow off the clunky vehicle. Once it was clear, Cal backed out of his parents' driveway and then cruised down the street, being mindful of the roads, which were well treated.

A few miles down the road, Cal stopped at a traffic light and shuffled through his car's center console to search for a CD. He wanted to listen to something edgy and angry to help ease his own frustration, but he couldn't find any of his rock albums. Instead, he withdrew his secret guilty pleasure—a Céline Dion Greatest Hits CD—and inserted the disc.

The stoplight turned green and Cal pressed the gas pedal, eager to get back to his apartment. Bittersweet violin strings began to resound through the car's speakers, soon accompanied by a gentle voice singing heartfelt lyrics. As the song continued, Cal was overcome with emotion while he pictured Andrew and Claire together, and he grew nauseous. As the powerful chorus commenced, Cal turned the volume up and began to sing along softly. Despite his greatest efforts to bury his sorrow, a single tear formed in his eye before it trickled down his cheek.

"What the fuck is this?" he exclaimed to himself as he wiped the tear away. Then, he was struck by a fit of borderline maniacal laughter. "I'm crying? I'm so pathetic."

The music continued for the remainder of Cal's drive home. When he arrived, he grabbed the CD from the car, headed into his cozy apartment, and changed into his pajamas. He had lied to his mother and didn't have anything to do at home. He'd just been longing to escape the melancholy.

Cal popped the Céline Dion disk into his CD player and then retrieved a bottle of wine from the fridge. Without needing a glass, Cal took a large gulp and then eased himself onto his couch. He had been through the worst heartbreak of his life three and a half years ago, and he had never gotten over Andrew, but now his former lover was with his baby sister. Cal shook his head in response to the ridiculousness of the situation and took another swig of wine.

Despite how hard he had tried to fight it, seeing Andrew had reignited the repressed feelings Cal still had for him—even after all those years—and he was just as distraught as he had been during the four months of their on again/off again college fling. Cal reflected on his bittersweet memories of Andrew as he continued to drink from the bottle of wine. Once it ran dry, Cal stumbled into the kitchen to retrieve another. He then plopped himself back on the couch and began sipping on the new bottle until he drank himself into a stupor.

Chapter Six

Despite the drowsing effect of the wine, Cal tossed and turned throughout the night, and by three o'clock that morning, he was wide awake—and still marginally drunk. Cal did not need to open the gym for another two and a half hours, but decided to head into work early since he couldn't sleep. Disoriented and dizzy from the previous night's binge, Cal opted to walk to work instead of driving. Wearing a pair of navy jogger pants, a black polyester hoodie, and a pair of worn training shoes, he stepped out into the cold morning air and began to stroll through the town.

The temperature was in the single digits at least—potentially below zero degrees—and a light dusting of snow coated the deserted roads while flurries continued to swirl in the moonlit sky. However, Cal was numb and ignored the frigid weather as the vapors of his breath floated aimlessly through the air. Despite still feeling tipsy, his mind was at ease and empty of any negative thoughts regarding Andrew as he walked through the tranquil silence of early morning.

When Cal arrived at the gym about twenty minutes later, he had little feeling left in his icy hands, but nevertheless remained cheery. He retrieved a set of keys from his pocket and then struggled to unlock the door with his frozen digits for a brief moment. Cal pushed the door open and slipped into the gym as the winter chill began growing painful in his bones while he sobered up a bit.

He traipsed over to his office in the back and tossed his keys and hoodie on the tidy desk. Cal grabbed his iPod from the office and then made his way back to the front desk, where he plugged it into the gym's music console and played his own choice of music, as opposed to the current pop hits the gym typically played. Electric guitars and a heavy drum rhythm pulsed through the speakers before the raspy voice of Joan Jett harmonized with the beat.

Cal nodded his head with the tempo as he stepped over to an empty rack and began loading the bar with various weight plates. Then, he lay on the cushioned bench, lifted the loaded bar off the handles, and lowered it to his chest before pressing the weight back up. He continued to perform bench presses, with each rep becoming sturdier and smoother. After several polished lifts, Cal completed the first set. He sat up and granted himself about a minute or so for a quick rest and then lay back on the bench to perform another set. Cal noticed his form was now much cleaner than it had been and was also surprised to discover how great he felt. His current state of slight grogginess left him serenely numb, which allowed him to power through his workout without getting fatigued.

After fifty minutes of various chest exercises, Cal decided to finish his workout with some cardio. He walked over to an empty row of cardio machines and stepped on a treadmill. Cal began jogging at a moderate pace and was once again amazed by his running performance; his breathing was steady; his legs were not at all sore, and he had barely broken a sweat. Cal increased the treadmill's speed by several levels and adjusted his pace to keep up with the machine. He was energized, and it seemed as if his stamina could not be depleted.

However, after about ten minutes of sprinting, Cal lost focus and his mind began to wander, becoming aware of every movement within his body: the slight churning in his stomach, the few beads of sweat trickling down his cool forehead, the tightness in his legs, the exhausted heartbeats pounding in his chest, and his wheezing gasps for air.

The welcoming numbness from the previous night's drinking binge had now worn off, leaving Cal susceptible to emotional and physical pain and weakness. His body was chilled, and he began to tremble from fatigue. He might be suffering from a panic attack, like the one he had experienced years ago after moving into his post-college apartment. He had been so alone and isolated then, feeling vulnerable and broken from his abysmal final semester. How different would his life have been if he had never met Andrew then? Would he have had better success in finding a meaningful connection with someone else? Would he have been happy for Claire when she brought Andrew home?

Caught up in his tiring ruminations, Cal's foot slipped on the treadmill, and he lost his balance. He fell backward and landed on his buttocks as the belt of the treadmill continued to race. Cal attempted to grab the machine's handrails as he fell, but it was futile and the speeding treadmill propelled Cal down its track before launching him off the machine. He collided headfirst into the wall behind him, and his vision began fading out to black.

"Cal?" a worried voice called out.

He moaned in response and opened his eyes as a blurry figure came into view. He gazed around in confusion until a dull ache in the back of his head reminded Cal of his fall. He shook his head and rubbed his eyes to discover Sophie standing over him.

"Cal, what happened?" she asked. "How long have you been here?"

"Ugh, what time is it?" Cal inquired feeling groggy.

"Whoa," she remarked and recoiled as she covered her nose. "Have you been drinking?"

"Pssh, no," he dismissed with a slight giggle. "Okay, maybe just a little."

"How much is just a little?"

"Do you mean how much I drank last night or this weekend?"

"Oh jeez," Sophie muttered under her breath before she helped Cal to his feet. "We're supposed to be opening in twenty minutes. Let's get you cleaned up."

Sophie led Cal across the empty gym and into the men's locker room. Then, she strode over to one of the showers and began running the hot water. Meanwhile, Cal slumped against a row of metal lockers and rubbed his forehead, which now throbbed.

"Why are hangovers a thing?" he mumbled.

"I'm guessing this is about Andrew?" Sophie reasoned as she tested the heat of the shower water. Cal nodded and avoided making eye contact. "Are you okay to stand on your own? You're not dizzy, right?"

"No, I'm not dizzy," he replied.

"All right, well, you're going to shower off and clean yourself up. Did you bring any clothes?"

"No, but I keep extras in my office."

"Okay, then get in the shower. I'll leave some clothes out for you, and then I'm going to run over to the bagel shop across the street and grab you something to eat. Sound good?"

Cal nodded gently and obeyed Sophie's instructions. Once she had left the locker room, Cal stepped into the shower and began washing with the courtesy soap and shampoo provided by the gym. As he washed his hair, Cal discovered a slight bump had formed on the back of his head, and he winced at its painful touch. When he was finished showering, he stepped out into the cold locker room and discovered a semi wrinkled black polo shirt and khaki chinos, along with a pair of compression shorts and socks. Cal grabbed a clean towel, dried himself off, and then dressed with haste. Reality had begun to sink in as his headache lessened and he realized it had to be past the gym's opening time.

As Cal exited the locker room, he glanced at the clock; it was almost six. He gazed around the gym, curious as to whether Sophie needed his help, and eyed several of the usual morning members who were working out. Upon a further sweep of the facility, he saw that it appeared to have already been prepared for opening. Cal furrowed his brow and then walked into his office and found a large cup of black coffee and a greasy breakfast sandwich waiting for him at his desk. Sophie was seated next to the desk, biting into a whole-grain bagel.

"Who opened the gym?" Cal wondered as he took a seat.

"I did," Sophie replied before she took another bite of her breakfast.

"Oh, thanks."

"No problem. I got you breakfast."

"Thanks," Cal said as he eyed the breakfast sandwich in suspicion. He wasn't nauseous at all; in fact, he was a bit hungry. However, Cal kept himself on a healthy, regimented meal plan, which centered on foods low in fat and high in protein. He rarely indulged in fatty foods, and considering what he had eaten—and drank—that weekend, Cal did not wish to sabotage his diet any further. Instead, he grabbed the cup of coffee and took a large gulp of the bitter drink.

"Eat the sandwich," Sophie instructed, sensing his apprehension and knowing how routine Cal could be with his eating.

"I can't. It'll ruin my abs—"

"Eat it," she interjected.

"Fine," Cal sighed. He rolled his eyes before taking an unwilling bite. As much as he hated to admit it, the greasy breakfast sandwich was delicious. The two sat in silence in Cal's office for several minutes as they ate.

"I didn't hear from you this weekend," Sophie said in a gentle voice as she wiped the corners of her mouth with a napkin. "How'd it go?"

"As well as could be expected," Cal replied, a hint of sarcasm in his voice.

"That good, huh?"

"It was really embarrassing."

"What happened?" Sophie inquired.

"Dinner was awful. My parents fawned over him, and I kept stammering like a fucking idiot," he groaned. "And then I got snowed in."

"You were snowed in?" she replied as her eyes widened in disbelief.

"For the entire weekend."

"Oh, Cal," Sophie said. "You were stuck at your parents' all weekend?"

"With *him*."

"So when did you get home?"

"Let's see," Cal recollected. "I left my parents' around five last night, got home a little before six, opened a bottle of wine, got drunk, belted out Céline Dion, and then passed out a couple hours later."

"You were singing Céline Dion songs?"

"No, I said *a* Céline Dion song...on repeat," he clarified.

"*My Heart Will Go On*?" Sophie guessed.

"*To Love You More*."

"Oh, jeez, this is bad," she stated.

"You think?" Cal snapped.

"And this whole weekend at your parents, you just acted like you had never met before?"

"Yep. We both did," Cal said. "Except, we kind of had a confrontation."

"What do you mean?"

"Well, I was hungover Saturday morning."

"Of course," Sophie added. Cal shot her a look, warning her to give him a break.

"Anyway, I went to go downstairs to get breakfast, and Andrew came out of the bathroom after his shower. And we kind of bumped into each other in the hallway."

"Was he naked?" Sophie blurted out. However, she noticed a glint of despair and longing in Cal's bloodshot eyes, and she retracted her question "Sorry. Um, so, did you guys talk?"

Cal sighed as he recollected his conversation with Andrew and that weekend's events, which he relayed to Sophie.

"Wow," she replied, once Cal had finished. "I'm not sure what to say."

"This is ridiculous," Cal exclaimed. "In my head, I know what Andrew and I had was nothing, but those feelings I had for him never really went away. I mean, he's...he's just...just a..."

"A fuckboy?" Sophie offered.

"Exactly! He's just a fuckboy," he agreed in frustration. "Or at least I thought he was. But after our talk, I'm starting to wonder if I was playing the victim card."

"What do you mean?"

"I've always put the blame on him, but what if it was my fault too? I was new to the whole dating thing back then, and I didn't know what to do or say. All those times of silence between us, I was always too nervous to text Andrew first. What if he was too?"

"Cal, it's dangerous to think like that. I mean, you've got to look at the entire situation between the two of you."

"But, he said—"

"Cal, you had sex with him, and then he left the next morning, and you never heard from him again. Not until now."

"I know," Cal replied in defeat. His demeanor suggested he wanted to say something more, but he remained silent as he stared blankly at his half-eaten breakfast sandwich.

"I know you've never really gotten over him, and I want to see you happy," Sophie began, "but I think too much has happened between you and Andrew for you guys to ever be together again. And even if you two did get back together, I don't think that would be good for you."

"I know," Cal repeated. He knew he and Andrew would never be together. All those years ago, when he had begun this love affair, Cal knew they would never be together. Now that his ex had ventured back into his life, all those feelings of desperate lust had resurfaced, and they were just as strong as ever. In fact, Cal felt transported back to that last semester of college when he had first fallen for Andrew, before being heartbroken. This time he was not back in Cal's life as a potential crush, or an ex-lover; he was now Claire's boyfriend. "But what do I do now that he's with Claire?"

"I really don't know," Sophie said. "From what you've told me, it sounds like things are pretty serious between Andrew and Claire. I think if you told her, you would be putting her in an awkward situation."

"But now I'm the one in an awkward situation."

"I know, but imagine if the tables were turned. How would you feel?"

"Yeah, you're right," Cal reasoned. "But what am I supposed to do? Keep pretending that nothing happened between us?"

"Maybe." Sophie shrugged, unsure as to what the appropriate course of action was.

"Trying to get over him..." he began in a shaky voice. A dry lump grew in Cal's throat, and he swallowed hard as he stood and walked over to a nearby window. "Trying to get over him has been hard enough to do for the past several years—without him in my life."

"I know. Believe me. I know," Sophie said. She joined Cal over by the window and rubbed his arm comfortingly. "I know how hard this was on you then, and I'm sure this must be hard to deal with now. But you're not the same person you were three and a half years ago."

"What do you mean?"

"You said you were new to dating when you first met Andrew. I remember, back when you told me you were seeing him, you were always so nervous and self-conscious around him," Sophie explained. "But, since then, I've seen you come into yourself. And you're in the best shape of your life right now."

"I guess so," Cal mumbled, unwilling to find anything positive about himself.

"Haven't you noticed how you've been carrying yourself lately? You're not the same scared twenty-one-year-old you were back then."

Sophie was right; Cal was in a much better state of mind, compared to when he had been involved with Andrew and the accompanying heartache that ensued upon graduation. Though he had often thought about his crush over the years and felt melancholic when reflecting on the time they had spent together, Cal had noticed his confidence returning, which he attributed to Sophie's company and his better-than-ever physique. Still, all he could do was nod in agreement.

"Come on, admit it! You're hot," she said with a smirk. "Now, maybe you can't be with Andrew, but show him what he missed out on. It's his turn to regret the past."

"Yeah, I guess you're right," Cal admitted with a chuckle.

"Of course I am," Sophie replied. "Now, finish eating, and then get to work. I'll cover for you."

"Thanks," he said as Sophie left him to his meal.

Cal sat in his silent office and finished his breakfast sandwich while he reflected on Sophie's encouraging remarks. Though what she said might have been true, it inspired little hope in Cal. How could he be hopeful for a positive outcome when the man who had haunted his heart for years reappeared in his life without warning?

Cal's headache continued to throb as an inevitable hangover began to settle over him. Fortunately, his greasy meal helped to ease his nausea. When Cal was done eating, he rubbed the growing lump on his head and then began his work for the day.

That Monday seemed to drag on for Cal, as he attempted to push thoughts of Andrew out of his mind so he could focus on his job. As the morning passed , his headache began to dissipate, although the painful bump on the back of his head remained and ached. By early afternoon, Cal's lack of sleep caused his eyelids to grow heavy. He struggled to stay awake as he filed various paperwork and responded to work-related emails. The rest of the afternoon was a blur, yet he was miraculously able to stay conscious. Around five, Sophie strolled into Cal's office and offered him a ride home, which he accepted with gratitude since he did not wish to walk home in the frigid weather.

As soon as Cal arrived at his apartment, he plopped onto his bed. Though his hangover had subsided hours ago, he was worn and off-kilter. The prospect that Andrew and Claire were a couple had shaken him to the core, and Cal's excessive drinking over the past few days did not help to relieve his emotional tension either.

I need to get my shit together. He couldn't let his yearning for Andrew destroy him, not again. Weary and emotional, Cal drifted into a deep slumber, which his body desperately needed.

Despite not setting his alarm, before passing out the night before, Cal still awoke at his usual time that morning. His body—though sore from his vigorous, drunken workout and fall—felt refreshed, and his mind was somewhat at ease, thanks to a much-needed good night's sleep. Cal rose out of bed—still dressed in the previous day's work clothes—and began his morning routine. After about forty-five minutes, he was prepared for the day ahead.

Cal attempted to feel optimistic about his current situation with Andrew as he stepped out of his apartment and into the bitter December chill. He crossed the slushy parking lot and retrieved his car keys from his coat pocket once he reached his beat-up car. Cal stepped into his aged vehicle and started up the engine before a muffled *pop* resonated from under the hood which was followed by dark wisps of smoke.

"Shit," Cal swore as he yanked the keys out of the ignition. He jumped out of his car and lifted its hood, releasing a thick cloud of smoke. Cal was no mechanical expert, but nevertheless scanned under the hood for telltale indications of malfunction; he assumed the hissing sound coming from the engine and the putrid scent of burned oil were not good signs. Cal retrieved his phone and called a nearby mechanic, who listed a handful of possible problems which could be responsible for his car troubles. Based upon the vehicle's maladies, the mechanic deemed it unsuitable for driving and instructed Cal to have the vehicle towed over to the shop, so he could conduct a proper inspection of the engine.

Cal dialed the number for a local towing company and then called Sophie, asking for a ride to work. As he waited in the blistery weather, Cal eyed his car sourly and cursed his bad luck until Sophie arrived to keep him company while they waited for the tow truck. After an additional twenty minutes or so, the truck pulled into the parking lot. A heavyset, middle-aged man with graying, untidied scruff climbed out from behind the driver's seat and approached Cal. He took his personal information and had Cal complete some forms before turning toward the still-smoking vehicle.

"Ha, this thing has seen better days," the truck driver chuckled as he prepped Cal's car for towing. "I doubt it'll be worth repairing."

"Gee, thanks," Cal retorted with his arms folded.

Once his vehicle had been towed, he settled himself into Sophie's car, and she drove them to work. She could sense Cal's tension and let him fume in silence. When they arrived at the gym, he sulked away to his office and slammed the door behind him, and then remained locked up with the door closed throughout the entire morning. Around early afternoon, Sophie decided she needed to check on her friend.

"Hey," she greeted as she peeked her head into the office. Cal was seated at his desk, with his back facing Sophie. "How's it going?"

"Fan-fucking-tastic," he replied, while remaining fixated on his computer.

"Oh," Sophie stated softly as she stepped in and then closed the door behind her. "Did you hear back from the mechanic?"

"Yep. He called about two hours ago."

"Um, what did he—"

"It's not worth repairing," Cal informed her. "I've been searching for cars online, but I'm not finding anything."

"Have you tried looking at—"

"Goddamn it!" Cal swore, which caused Sophie to jump. He slammed his mouse upon the desk and shoved his monitor away from himself in disgust. "Everything online is a piece of shit, or way out of my price range. This is just ridiculous!"

"Cal."

"Goddamn piece of shit car dying on me."

"Cal."

"Fucking mechanic probably doesn't even know what he's talking about."

"Cal!" she exclaimed. He fell silent and Sophie gazed at her disheveled friend with a worried expression on her face. "Cal, breathe. Take a deep breath. We'll figure this out."

Cal pinched the bridge of his nose as he attempted to calm himself. "I'm sorry. I know it's only a car, and it can be replaced. But now, with everything going on..." he trailed off as his voice grew shaky. "It's just really bad timing; that's all."

"It'll be okay," Sophie reassured him as she strode around the desk and gave Cal a tight hug. "This will all be okay. I'll drive you to work this week, and then we can shop for cars this weekend."

"You don't have to do that."

"I know, but I want to. It'll be fun, and we can make a day out of it."

"You sure?" Cal asked, not wanting to be a burden.

"Of course I'm sure! Besides, it'll help take my mind off the fact that my parents are going on a cruise for Christmas *without* me."

"What?!"

"I know!" Sophie stated. "They're leaving Friday, and won't be back till after New Year's Eve."

"What are you going to do for the holidays?" he wondered. "Are you gonna try to stay with Rich's family?"

"I don't know. His family doesn't do anything for Christmas," she said.

"Well, you know you're always welcome to come to my parents' house. We're having my mom's side of the family over this year."

"Thanks, I'll keep that in mind," Sophie replied. "I've got a client coming in for a training session in a few, but we can work out the car shopping details later."

"Okay, sounds good," Cal said. "Hey, Sophie?"

"Yeah?" she replied, standing at his office door.

"Thanks," he smiled.

"You don't need to thank me," Sophie replied, returning his smile. "You know I'll always be here for you."

Chapter Seven

The rest of the dismal work week passed by and was otherwise uneventful. Though his job had provided a slight distraction from Andrew, Cal welcomed the upcoming weekend. He and Sophie had made plans to go car shopping that Saturday, which helped alleviate Cal's near-constant stress. Due to his car's untimely demise, he had to rely on a rental vehicle, and he was eager to drive a set of wheels belonging to him again.

Cal tidied up his desk and snuck out of the office early since he had finished everything he needed to accomplish that week. He hurried to his rental vehicle—a classy, silver car which was a year old—and glanced at its clock once he had started the engine: 5:20 p.m.

I've got plenty of time to get ready for tonight, he determined.

Cal had been talking with someone online for a couple of weeks, and the two had made plans to meet for dinner at seven that night. The guy appeared handsome in his pictures and seemed normal, yet Cal was not anticipating the date. In fact, he couldn't remember the last time he had felt excitement at the prospect of going out with someone other than Andrew. Cal sighed and then drove out of the parking garage.

He got caught in some traffic on his commute home and arrived at his apartment just after a quarter to six. He traipsed into his bedroom, stripped out of his business casual attire, down to his briefs, and then sifted through his dresser as he searched for something to wear, not that he really cared since this date probably wouldn't lead to anything worthwhile. After several moments, he retrieved a pair of stylish, ripped jeans and a red-and-gray, three-quarter-sleeve Henley shirt and got dressed. Afterward, he shuffled over to the bathroom mirror, assessed his appearance, and then applied a few subtle spritzes of cologne.

Cal took one last glance at the mirror and had to admit he didn't look half bad. Cal appreciated his own features, though he rarely acknowledged that for fear of being regarded as conceited. However, despite his positive perception of his appearance that night, he was uncomfortable. Cal would have preferred to be dressed in a pair of sweatpants and a baggy T-shirt and enjoy a quiet evening at home by himself. He had no desire to go on this date, but it was too short notice to cancel. So, Cal mustered what little positivity and excitement he had and departed for his date.

The two had arranged to meet at a local sports bar and grill, and Cal pulled up to the location right on time. As he walked to the entrance, he spotted his date standing outside the front door. He looked exactly like he had online, which was a pleasant surprise; nothing was worse than going on a date with someone who did not resemble their pictures. As Cal approached the restaurant, he caught his date's eye.

"Hi," Cal greeted with a warm smile before he extended his hand. "I'm Cal. Nice to finally meet you."

"Hi. I'm Jacob," his date replied as he shook Cal's hand. "Nice to meet you too."

Even though Cal had been talking to Jacob online for a couple of weeks and knew his name, he still liked to introduce himself on the first date to make things seem a little more personal instead of going out with a stranger from a dating app.

He and Jacob made small talk as they entered the restaurant, and were soon seated at a cozy booth. After their waitress took their drink order, Cal eyed Jacob from across the table. He sported a fashionable undercut, with his tawny hair parted neatly to the side. His light-blue eyes conveyed genuine expression with strong facial features and a clean-shaven chin. His overall dapper appearance was complemented by a slender, yet muscular physique similar to Cal's, though Jacob may have been a half a size larger. He was definitely attractive, and yet Cal felt *nothing*.

Cal's heart did not skip a beat, he didn't stumble over his words, and no butterflies fluttered in his stomach. There was simply no attraction there. And why was that? Why could Cal not feel anything for the handsome man sitting across from him, yet he could fall so carelessly for Andrew, who was so average and unavailable? Cal attempted to suppress his dark musings and returned his attention to his date. Maybe he just needed to get to know Jacob better, and then he would feel something.

Cal found it easy to converse with the young man, who was quite amiable. Jacob was two years older than Cal, a successful banking manager, and family oriented. The two discovered they shared many similar interests and continued to chat with ease throughout dinner. As they finished their meals, Cal experienced a tinge of guilt. The date was going well, and he enjoyed Jacob's company, but he only felt a platonic connection; he was unsure if he could feel anything more. However, the charming smile Jacob gave Cal insinuated that he may have begun to develop feelings—feelings that Cal may not be able to reciprocate.

When the waitress arrived with the check, Cal reached for his wallet, but Jacob snatched the bill off the table. Cal offered to pay for dinner and drinks, or even split it, but Jacob objected and insisted on covering it, much to Cal's annoyance since he hated when his dates paid for him—especially when Cal only had lukewarm feelings. Nevertheless, Cal thanked Jacob in an attempt to appreciate his kindness.

After the check had been paid, the two grabbed their coats and left the restaurant. They continued their conversation as they crossed the semideserted parking lot, and Jacob pulled out his phone to check the time.

"You know," he began as he pocketed his phone, "it's only a little after nine, if you wanted to grab a drink or go to a movie or something."

"Oh, I wish I could," Cal lied, "but I have to get up early tomorrow to shop for cars with my friend."

"Oh, are you thinking of getting a new car?" Jacob asked.

"Yeah, I have to. Mine died on me this week, and I've been stuck with a rental," he explained.

"Aw, I'm sorry to hear that."

"It was a long time coming, I guess. It just happened at a really inconvenient time."

"Well, good luck tomorrow," Jacob said as he walked with Cal to the rental vehicle.

"Thanks," he replied with a grin as he approached the driver's side of the car.

"I had a lot of fun tonight," Jacob stated before taking a step closer to Cal.

"Me too," he said as he grabbed the car keys out of his pocket. "I'm glad we did this."

As Cal was about to unlock the door, he sensed Jacob moving closer. The two men gazed into each other's eyes, and Jacob gave him *the look* before he tilted his head.

Oh shit, Cal thought as he prepared himself for the kiss. He didn't want to lead Jacob on, but he also did not want to pull away and hurt him. Maybe Cal didn't want to pull away for another reason; maybe he hoped this kiss would induce some type of romantic feeling within him.

He tilted his own head and closed his eyes once their lips connected. Jacob gave him a soft and tender kiss, with his mouth slightly open. The very subtle stubble of an otherwise smooth face scratched Cal's chin as he continued to press his lips against Jacob's. This lasted for a moment longer before the two broke away mutually.

"I'll text you tomorrow," Jacob offered with a flirtatious smile.

"Sounds good," Cal replied. "Have a good night."

"Thanks! You too!" he waved before he crossed the parking lot to his own car.

Cal settled himself inside his rental car as an increased feeling of guilt came over him. Jacob seemed like a great guy; he was handsome, he had a great personality, and he was looking for a relationship. He and Cal had a lot in common, and the kiss was great. Still, Cal felt nothing. Had Andrew damaged Cal so deeply he could never feel the excitement of a first date again? Or was Cal not allowing himself to fall for someone other than Andrew? These thoughts weighed upon Cal as he drove home and later haunted his dreams.

The next morning, Cal awoke around eight and promptly got out of bed since Sophie had planned on meeting at his place around ten to go car shopping. Cal ate a light breakfast, showered, and readied himself for the day ahead. Once Sophie arrived, Cal drove them in the rental vehicle across town to check out the first car shop on their list.

They eyed the lot's used inventory, but Cal was somewhat disappointed by the selection. While the cars were in his price range, most of them were *very* used and not much of an improvement from his prior vehicle. Cal strolled down the aisles and attempted to avoid making eye contact with any of the salespeople, since he had no intention of purchasing any of the cars on display.

When Cal's cell phone started to vibrate in his pocket, he instinctively reached to retrieve it. He frowned when he received a text from Jacob, saying that he had such a great time at dinner and wanted to get together again.

"Is everything okay?" Sophie asked when she saw Cal's grim expression. "Who is it?"

"Jacob," he said as he pocketed his phone without replying.

"Is that the guy you've been talking to online?"

"Yep. We went out to dinner last night," Cal informed her.

"How did it go?"

"He's funny and nice and successful," he said. "And he's really hot."

"Oh, that's great!" Sophie exclaimed.

"And I think he likes me," Cal added.

"Then, why the face?" she wondered while they inspected a beige car with a dented bumper. "What did his text say?"

"He said he had a lot of fun last night, and he wants to hang out again soon," he sighed.

"That's a good thing, isn't it?"

"You would think so, right?"

"You don't like him," Sophie said, rather than asked.

"I don't know," he confessed. "Probably not. I don't know what's wrong with me."

"Cal, nothing is wrong with you. You can't expect to like every single guy you go out with."

"I know, but I never expected to not like any of the guys I've gone out with," Cal replied in frustration. "It's like I haven't had feelings for anyone since—"

"Andrew," she finished.

"Yeah," he said. "And then, along comes Jacob. He's good-looking and we get along, and he has a job and cares about family too; he's perfect on paper. He's a catch—especially compared to some of the crazies I've gone out with. So why can't I feel anything?"

"I think you're putting too much pressure on yourself to have things work out," Sophie reasoned. "You're allowed to go out with someone and not have feelings for them."

"I know, but...this happens with everyone I go out with. I don't know if I'm going out with the wrong guys, or if I'm doing something wrong—if I'm not letting myself fall for anyone else."

"Maybe you just need some time to yourself and avoid dating," Sophie offered.

"You're probably right," Cal concurred. "But whatever I do, I can't win. If I don't date, then I wallow at home because I'm single and regret that I took that job and never got to be with Andrew. Or, if I do date, I focus on all the guy's flaws and ways that he's not Andrew, and then I'm miserable I'm not with him."

"I think if you date someone for a while and give it some time, then you'll be able to forget about Andrew."

"But I'm afraid I'll date someone for a while and still won't have any feelings for them. And I don't want to lead anyone on."

"Well, you can't always worry about that," Sophie insisted. "Sometimes you have to focus on yourself and your feelings."

"But I don't want to be Andrew because that's exactly what he did," Cal countered.

"Well don't be a douchebag, obviously. But you can't always worry about things working out or someone else's feelings. You need to pay attention to what feels right to you too."

"I know," he said, and then glanced around at several nearby cars.

"So, are you gonna see Jacob again?" Sophie questioned.

"I'm not sure yet," he admitted with a slight sigh. "This place sucks though. Let's go check out somewhere else."

Cal and Sophie drove over to another car dealership about ten minutes down the road. Unlike the last lot, this one possessed a larger assortment of vehicles, ranging from very affordable yet semi-worn cars to pricier, newer models. Cal walked into the office and spoke with a car dealer while Sophie wandered through the lot, scrutinizing the various vehicles.

The car dealer began to walk Cal through his inventory, showcasing models that were in Cal's budget and with decent mileage. There were several vehicles that appealed to him, both in terms of specifications and appearance. After a while, Cal had set his sights on a modest dark-blue car that was a few years old.

"Hey, Cal," Sophie called.

"Yeah," he responded, and began walking toward her.

"I think you should get this one," she said with a chuckle as she gestured to the vehicle she had been eyeing. It was a sleek midnight-black sports car with tinted windows and luxurious silver rims.

"Ha, I wish," he replied as he inspected under the hood of the vehicle that appeared to be pristine and well-maintained. "How much is it?"

"Twenty-seven thousand," Sophie informed him as she read the tag on the vehicle. "It's two years old and only has thirty thousand miles on it. That's not a bad price for this."

"Too bad it's just a *little* out of my price range," he reminded her.

"So? You've already paid off your student loans; treat yourself," she teased.

"Maybe I'll treat myself in ten years when I've got a little bit more of a financial cushion," Cal reasoned. "Come on. I think I actually did find a car—one I can afford."

He and Sophie strolled over to the car dealer and arranged to take the dark-blue car out for a test drive. It may not have been as sexy as the sleek sports vehicle, but it drove well and had a polished finish and classy appearance about it that was certainly an upgrade from his last vehicle.

When they returned to the lot, Cal was satisfied with the test drive and was ready to purchase the car. He went back into the office and spoke to the dealer, who informed him that the paperwork for the vehicle was filed at their satellite company in the next town over, and they would need to have it sent to their office from the other location.

Since the dealership was going to be closed on Sunday, Cal arranged a time on Monday after work to purchase the vehicle.

While Cal was there, he wrote out a check to place a deposit and then left with Sophie. Car shopping had gone much quicker than anticipated, and since it was just past noon, the two decided to go out to lunch. As Cal drove to their favorite Chinese restaurant, his phone began buzzing in his pocket. He waited until he reached a red traffic light to retrieve it, but by that time the call had already gone to his voicemail, and vibrated once more to notify him that someone had left a message.

"Can you check who it is?" Cal asked as he handed his phone over to Sophie, without glancing at its screen.

Sophie took it and began to listen to the voicemail. When the light turned green, Cal pressed the gas and continued toward the restaurant. He couldn't identify the muffled voice playing over the voicemail, but in his peripheral vision, he could see Sophie's face drop.

"Don't tell me it's Jacob," Cal grimaced.

"No, it's work," she stated in disbelief. "Something happened; we need to get over there now."

"Shit," he swore before he made a quick U-turn and sped toward the gym.

When they arrived, Cal parked right next to the curb, ignoring the "no parking" sign. He and Sophie hurried out of the car and were greeted by emergency vehicles and the owner of the facility.

"This can't be good," Sophie said aloud before they reached the gym entrance.

"Hey, guys," the owner greeted in a grim tone.

"Mr. Banks, what happened?" Cal asked.

"A pipe burst in one of the upstairs locker rooms."

"How bad is it?" Sophie wondered.

"The locker room was flooded, and some of the equipment below it was damaged," Mr. Banks informed them. "We're going to need to tear up the floor upstairs to see how bad the damage is. Plus, all the equipment will need to be assessed to see what needs to be replaced."

"How long is that going to take?" Cal inquired.

"At least two weeks. We're closing down the gym till then, and we'll extend the closure if need be," he stated. "Don't worry though. It'll be counted as paid time off for the employees, and it won't be deducted from their vacation days. But, Cal, I need your help, and I'm sorry to ask you this on your day off."

"No worries, what can I do?" he asked.

"Can you work on an email to send out to all the clients, and set up an automated phone message letting them know about the closure?" Mr. Banks requested. "The staff also needs to be informed."

"Sure thing. I'll get started on that," Cal replied.

Just after three o'clock, Cal and Sophie finished notifying clients and employees alike of the gym's untimely closure. By then, the two friends were too exhausted from a long day of browsing cars and handling a work crisis to go out to eat. Instead, they drove back to Cal's apartment and then parted ways.

Having not eaten since that morning, Cal was starving and headed into his kitchen to prepare a quick meal. However, as he reached for the fridge, his phone began buzzing once again. He pulled it out from his pocket, in case it was a work-related call, but discovered it was his mother.

"Hey, Mom," Cal answered, in a somewhat disgruntled voice, before he turned his attention back to the fridge.

"Gee, don't sound too excited," Mrs. Adams remarked.

"Sorry, I had a rough day," he apologized as he retrieved a chicken breast and some vegetables.

"Aw, what's wrong?"

"My car died on me Monday, so Sophie and I went to look at some cars today, but then we got a call from work and a pipe burst and flooded the locker room."

"What is this? I don't see you for a week and all this happens?" his mother exclaimed. "How bad is it at the gym?"

"Pretty bad," Cal grumbled and grabbed a frying pan from the dish rack. "It's going to be closed for at least two weeks."

"Oh no! What are you going to do then?" she wondered.

"I don't know; hang around here, I guess. Mr. Banks is giving paid time off for the closure."

"That's good that you're still getting paid during this," Mrs. Adams stated.

"Yeah, I guess," Cal replied. "Mom, I was just getting ready to cook some dinner for myself. Did you need something, or can I call you back to chat when I'm done?"

"Well, I was really calling to see what your plans were next week for Christmas."

"Oh, um, I'm not sure."

"You know, Claire and Andrew are coming to stay with us for the whole week leading up to Christmas."

"Yeah, I remember you saying that," Cal said as calmly as possible.

"You should stay with us too," his mother reasoned.

There it is.

"We have the extra guest bedroom, and it would be nice to have the family together," Mrs. Adams continued. "Plus, I could use the extra help before the rest of our clan comes in for Christmas Day."

"Well, I don't know if I can, Mom."

"Why not? You just said the gym is going to be closed for the next two weeks."

"But Mr. Banks might need me," he countered.

"So what will you be doing while you wait for him since he *might* need you?"

"I don't know. I'll just lie low here and...read," Cal lied.

"You're going to stay cooped up in your apartment to read for two weeks before Christmas? Cal, that's not healthy."

"Mom, I've got other things to do—"

"I'm making a nice dinner on Monday for when Claire and Andrew get here—"

"And I've got errands to run—"

"It'll be so nice having everyone together—"

"But, Mom—"

"Okay, I'll see you next Monday at six. Bye!" His mother hung up, leaving Cal alone in his kitchen which was silent other than the sizzling chicken and vegetables in the frying pan. At twenty-five years old, Cal was still amazed at how his mother was always able to get the last word in.

He turned his attention back to the stove and finished cooking his meal, although his appetite had subsided. The thought of having to be in the same house as Andrew for an entire week caused Cal's anxiety to spike, leaving his stomach in knots. He set the chicken and vegetables aside and decided to save it for later as his face flushed and his hands shook due to his nerves.

Cal strode to the sink in the bathroom and splashed some cold water on his face. He took a deep breath as he attempted to calm himself. After several moments, his body grew steadier and his complexion returned to normal. Still, he grasped the bathroom counter for support as he took another stabilizing breath.

"You're okay. You're okay," Cal reassured himself, though his stomach continued to churn with anxiety, and his eyes stung like they could form tears. However, he refused to allow a single tear to escape from his gray eyes. He could not allow himself to feel weakened by Andrew again. Instead, he gazed ahead at himself in the mirror. It was funny, since a week ago, he had observed how Andrew's physical appearance had altered slightly over the past three years. Now that Cal was staring at himself in the mirror, he wondered how much his own appearance had changed.

His medium-length, dark-brown hair was much the same as it had been when he and Andrew had met, but that was the only real similarity. His then slim body was now toned and muscular, and the beard he had been growing throughout the last semester of college had been stripped and replaced by a clean-shaven face. However, inspecting himself in the mirror, Cal realized he hated everything he saw.

He was tired of having the same haircut. He disliked how his smooth complexion created a sense of innocence and youthfulness in his face. He was unsatisfied with how his clothing merely hung on his body as opposed to complementing it. Sophie's words rang through his ears:

You're not the same person you were three and a half years ago. You're not the same scared twenty-one-year-old you were back then. Come on, admit it! You're hot! It's his turn to regret the past.

Cal wanted to change. He was bored with his appearance and wanted to create a new version of himself—a *better* version of himself. He wanted to create a new, desirable image that would make anyone envious. The next time Andrew saw him, Cal wanted to leave him drooling and kicking himself in the ass for letting him get away. The next time Andrew saw him, Cal wouldn't be a bumbling idiot dressed in his father's ill-fitting hand-me-downs. No, the next time Andrew saw him, Cal would be a vengeful ghost, haunting his ex with the memories of what could've been.

It's his turn to regret the past.

"Fuck you, Andrew," Cal spat.

Chapter Eight

Despite the gym's closure and having two weeks of paid time off, Cal still awoke by six o'clock Monday morning. Even on his usual days off, Cal rarely slept past eight and was more productive by waking up at an earlier hour. Today, however, he had much to accomplish, so he welcomed the annoying chirp of his alarm clock, and he rolled out of bed with ease. That morning marked the commencement of Cal's transformation, his recreation, and it was a change he was eager to make.

Cal ate a light breakfast, changed into his training shorts and a compression shirt, and drove over to a community gym; he was not going to miss a workout simply because his usual gym was closed. Working out was almost therapeutic for Cal, who believed that exerting himself helped to build a sturdy foundation both physically and emotionally. That morning, though, his workout was much more rewarding.

With every weight Cal lifted, it seemed as though he lifted another emotional weight of Andrew off his chest. With every muscle Cal activated, he felt as though he amplified its growth to better entice Andrew. The thought of his ex groveling after seeing his soon-to-be updated appearance made Cal smile, and it motivated him to push himself through his exercises.

After completing his workout, Cal departed from the gym feeling accomplished and headed home briefly since he still had several errands to run. Cal showered and then—still wrapped in his towel—retrieved his phone to schedule a hair appointment. Usually, he went to the local barbershop down the road, because all he had needed in the past was a quick trim, and the barber was cheap. However, Cal did not want a simple touch-up today. What he needed was a whole new hairstyle.

He searched online for various hair salons in his area. After several minutes, he found a pricier, upscale place with many positive reviews, and he dialed the number. A bubbly receptionist answered after the first ring and searched through her appointment book for an opening. She flipped through several pages and then discovered one of the stylists would be available the next morning shortly after the salon opened. Cal booked the appointment and thanked the receptionist before he hung up.

Then, he called the car dealership he and Sophie had browsed over the weekend. When the salesman answered, Cal asked if he could come in earlier than scheduled to finalize the paperwork for the car, since he no longer had to work. The salesman had no objections, and he and Cal agreed on meeting in an hour. After he ended the call, Cal removed his towel and dressed himself. Upon seeing himself in the mirror, he frowned. Cal was not a bad dresser by any means, but he felt frumpy in his current wardrobe. He decided he would stop at a nearby department store to purchase some new clothes after he was finished at the car dealership.

Just as Cal was about to leave to pick up his car, his phone vibrated; it was Jacob.

> *Hey handsome! Hope you had a great rest of your weekend! I was wondering if you wanted to grab drinks tonight?*

Cal rolled his eyes and shoved the phone in his pocket, without answering. Despite his conversation with Sophie on Saturday, he was still uncertain about how to handle this situation with Jacob. Cal did not know if he had genuine feelings for him, and he did not want to lead Jacob on. No matter how great Jacob seemed, he could not compare to Andrew and the fact that Cal was attempting to show how much better off he was without Andrew did not help to keep his former flame off his mind. Cal sighed and figured he'd think Jacob's offer over on his way to the car dealership before he made a decision; he wanted to say yes, but thought he should say no.

When Cal arrived at the lot, he saw the modest, dark-blue car he would be purchasing, which had been parked right next to the dealer's office. He stepped out of the rental vehicle—which he had arranged to be picked up by the rental company at that location—and was hit with the brisk weather. As Cal crossed the lot toward the office, the sleek, midnight-black sports car caught his eye. He hurried into the office to escape the chill of December and greeted the salesman with a firm handshake before they began the process of completing the necessary paperwork for his new car.

About thirty minutes later, Cal walked out of the dealer's office with his keys. He stepped into his new vehicle and proudly drove out of the lot, heading toward the mall. However, he did not drive away in the modest blue vehicle. Instead, he had splurged and purchased the sleek, midnight-black sports car with tinted windows and luxurious, silver rims. He knew it might be foolish to have bought a car that was somewhat out of his price range since it was considered a depreciating asset and—being only twenty-five—he was on a budget. However, Cal was never one to spend money in a frivolous manner, and he saved a considerable portion of every paycheck. While he had spent more on this sexy sports car than he had intended, he knew he still had enough money saved to cover his bills for the next year, as well as any other unforeseeable costs that may appear in the immediate future.

Screw being practical, Cal thought giddily as he cruised down the highway toward the mall. Yes, it was important to be frugal, but what good was it to have additional money saved if he wasn't going to spend some of it?

With the recent appearance of his ex and the accompanying emotional baggage, Cal had come to the conclusion he needed to focus on himself and do what made him happy, whether it was practical or not. And Sophie was right in her assertion that he needed to pay attention to what felt right to him and not always worry about someone else's feelings.

These realizations continued to ruminate in Cal's mind as he arrived at the mall, and once he parked in the crowded parking lot, he pulled out his phone. Cal texted Jacob and told him he was unable to go out for drinks, but he'd be available to get together the following night. Jacob replied a few minutes later, saying he would also be free the following evening, and the two texted on and off while Cal shopped for a new wardrobe.

Cal arrived at his apartment complex around midafternoon, with his new car and multiple shopping bags filled with assorted stylish apparel. He was exhausted from a busy day of running around and weaving through crowds of Christmas shoppers for a couple of hours at the mall. He plopped his shopping bags in his bedroom, and—while his bank account was drastically emptier—he was fulfilled for a moment. He was pleased with his purchases, and this retail therapy seemed to ease any apprehension he may have had about spending Christmas with Andrew.

Cal fixed himself a quick sandwich and then shuffled over to his computer. As he ate his late lunch, he browsed through various trendy hairstyles and saved pictures of cuts he liked. After he had selected several hairstyles, Cal spent the rest of the day lounging around his apartment and getting some much-needed relaxation.

The next morning, he woke at his usual time and headed over to his temporary gym for another daily workout; he did his routine cardio exercises and then chose to work his leg muscles. After Cal was finished at the gym, he returned to his apartment, showered, and then dressed in clean clothes in preparation for his hair appointment.

A few minutes after nine, Cal drove over to the salon, arriving ten minutes before his appointment time. While he waited in the salon's lounge, Cal scrolled through various pictures of trendy men's hairstyles, which he had saved on his phone. Several minutes later, a young stylist named Sky—with metallic blonde hair styled in a choppy bob—entered the lounge and called Cal's name. He followed Sky back into the suave salon and took a seat at her work station. Cal consulted with her about what type of hairstyle he was interested in and referenced the pictures on his phone. After a few minutes of conversation, the two confirmed what Cal wanted and Sky went to work.

She started by rinsing Cal's hair with warm water and massaging an exfoliating conditioner into his scalp.

Afterward, Sky dried his hair with a blow drier and then retrieved her hair-cutting tools. She ran an electric razor along the sides and back of Cal's head and shaved his hair away at various lengths. Next, she took a pair of shears and trimmed his top until an inch or two of hair had been chopped off. Once the stylist finished trimming his hair, she grabbed a razor blade and cleaned up the edges of Cal's hairline around his ears and the back of his neck. Lastly, she took a small amount of wax, which she ran through Cal's hair and styled it.

"All finished," Sky announced in a chipper voice as she spun Cal around to face the mirror. "What do you think?"

He gazed into the mirror and eyed his hair. The sides were skintight and faded, starting at practically stubble length at his hairline before increasing in length to the top of his head. The once medium-length hair was now noticeably shorter and was fashioned into a stylish faux hawk, using just enough hair product so it retained a natural look.

"I love it," Cal replied with a smile, and he ran a hand along the smooth side—practically identical to the picture he had shown Sky. He thanked the stylist and tipped her generously before he left the salon satisfied.

Later that day, Cal and Jacob finalized the details for their date that night, deciding to go to see a movie. When the time came for Cal to prepare for their date, he was indifferent. For once, he wasn't thinking about Andrew, which he welcomed. However, he wasn't certain he felt any sort of excitement over the idea of going out with Jacob again. Cal was more hopeful this date might allow him to feel something to determine what feelings—if any—he might have.

As Cal went to grab his coat, he stopped in front of the bathroom mirror to check his hair one more time and smiled at his reflection; he liked his new hairstyle and thought it enhanced his appearance. When he finished staring at himself, he threw on his coat, left his apartment, and drove over to the movie theater, where he met Jacob by the entrance.

"Oh, I didn't realize it was you at first," Jacob commented as Cal strode toward him in the brisk evening air. "New haircut?"

"Ha ha, yeah," he replied as he received a hug from his date.

"It looks great. Very handsome," Jacob complimented.

"Thanks," Cal smiled. "Let's head inside. It's freezing out here."

The two men entered the movie theater and purchased tickets for a big-budget action film that Cal paid for this time. They headed into the somewhat empty theater and sat in the very last row of abandoned seats. Cal and Jacob conversed before the lights dimmed and the movie began.

Cal found himself engrossed in the film, which was comprised of an original storyline and critically acclaimed acting. About thirty minutes into the movie, Jacob's hand brushed up against his on the armrest of the chair. He opened his hand and clasped Jacob's, and he in turn gently stroked Cal's hand with his thumb. He stared into Jacob's eyes, which twinkled as he smiled, and then Cal leaned in and kissed him. For the most part, he was not interested in any sort of public displays of affection—even hand-holding. However, since the theater was practically deserted and there was no one in their near vicinity, Cal dismissed his apprehension as he and Jacob continued to kiss.

After several moments, the two broke apart and resumed watching the movie while still holding hands. Cal's heart raced and a warm rush surged through his body, which surprised him. Was he developing feelings for Jacob? Could he maybe actually like him? Cal smiled while he held Jacob's hand for the remainder of the movie. However, once the film ended he let go of his hand, and they exited the theater.

"So," Jacob began as they stepped outside, "I live right around the block. If it's not too late, want to stop by for a drink?"

"Yeah, sounds good," Cal answered without overthinking his decision for once. The two men stepped into their separate cars, and Cal followed Jacob back to his place.

They parked in a well-lit lot next to the modernized, garden-style apartments, and then hurried upstairs to Jacob's flat on the second floor, eager to escape the winter chill.

"What can I get you to drink?" he inquired, as he hung his coat in the closet.

"Beer is fine," Cal replied before gazing around. The apartment was sleek and tidily decorated, almost resembling a cozy office space. Still, it had a charming and comfortable feel to it. "You have a great apartment."

"Oh, thank you," Jacob smiled as he entered the living room with two glass bottles and handed one to Cal. "I've been here a few years now. I like the location."

"Yeah, it seems like it's in a pretty convenient place, being only a few blocks from the main street. Thanks," Cal added as he took his beer before Jacob tilted his own bottle upward.

"Cheers," he grinned, and clinked his bottle with Cal's. Then, the two men settled themselves on the sleek leather couch and conversed as they sipped their beverages.

As Cal reached the bottom of his bottle, he sensed an ever so slight twinge of tipsiness grow inside him. He was no lightweight, so what was the cause of his buzz? Was it the fact that he hadn't eaten in several hours? Perhaps he was more conscious of his level of sobriety since he was drinking with a date and not a friend. Regardless, Cal finished the last bit of his drink and placed the empty bottle on a nearby end table.

"Do you want another?" Jacob asked.

"No, I'm good, but thanks," he replied.

"You sure?"

"Yeah," Cal said as Jacob took a last swig of beer before he set his own empty bottle to the side. Then, the two men made eye contact, and Cal could not suppress a semi-flirty smile. Jacob returned the smile and slid across the couch to move closer to his date. He placed his hand on the back of Cal's head and leaned in for a passionate kiss.

Cal wrapped his arms around Jacob's welcoming body, and the two men embraced as they continued to kiss. Jacob's plump lips traveled from Cal's mouth to his cheek, earlobe, and neck. He reclined back on the couch and exhaled with pleasure as Jacob positioned himself over Cal.

"You're really freaking cute," he remarked as he stroked Cal's stubbly cheek with his fingers. "And I like your scruff."

"Thanks," Cal laughed. "And you're really freaking cute too."

They gazed into each other's eyes meaningfully for a moment and then resumed kissing. They held each other close as their passionate embrace grew tighter. Cal's heart pounded and his groin stiffened with excitement, as his body responded to Jacob's romantic touch. He realized his mind was completely at ease—without reflecting on ghosts from the past—as a giddy sense of contentment settled over him. Cal was beginning to think he actually liked Jacob, which excited him.

When was the last time I felt this way? Since Andrew?

Cal dismissed this thought, unwilling to be reminded of the painful past, as Jacob eased himself off the couch. He stood and lifted Cal, who then wrapped his arms and legs around him. The two continued to kiss as Jacob carried him to the bedroom, and he plopped Cal onto the bed before pulling off his shirt.

Cal smiled as he discarded his own shirt, and Jacob hugged him tightly as he sank onto the bed next to him. Cal's arousal—both physically and emotionally—increased by the intimate warmth generated as their soft skin pressed against each other. They lay facing side by side on the cozy bed and wrapped in a tender embrace. Jacob gazed into Cal's gray eyes and grinned.

"Did I already tell you you're really freaking cute?"

"Hmm, you might've mentioned it," Cal laughed as Jacob held his hand and kissed him on the forehead.

"Well, it's true," he stated.

"Aw, thank you. You're really handsome," Cal complimented.

"Thanks." Cal and Jacob cuddled in peaceful silence, completely at ease and enjoying each other's company. Cal fondled a tuft of Jacob's light chest hair while Jacob caressed Cal's arm. In his relaxed state, Cal found himself growing drowsy, but he continued to accept gentle, soft kisses from Jacob. Soon, the kisses intensified, and Cal's passion was reignited.

The two were lip-locked, and Cal stroked Jacob's nipple. He responded by groping Cal's rump and then rubbed his crotch. Cal's lips broke away to release a pleasurable moan as he rolled onto his back, welcoming Jacob's touch. He climbed over Cal and began kissing his neck, chest, and nipples as he gradually worked his way down to his waist. Cal continued to emit sensual groans as he ran his fingers through Jacob's hair.

Cal did not believe in casual sex and always strived to save sexual acts for relationships. Despite this belief and his lack of relationships, he had hooked up on occasion in the past, though he was not proud of those encounters. Normally, Cal would not let things progress this far on a second date, but something was different with Jacob. Cal believed he had feelings for him and wanted to continue seeing him in the future. Therefore, he welcomed Jacob's exploration and appreciation of his body.

Jacob undid the button to Cal's jeans and glanced up for nonverbal consent as his fingers played with the waistband of his briefs. Cal accepted his advances as he slid his pants off. Jacob kneeled over him and ran his hands over Cal's body as their lips met. Cal caressed his toned body until Jacob broke away. He kissed Cal's waist for a moment before he turned his attention toward his exposed, erect penis. Jacob tantalized his skin as he ran his sensuous tongue around the base before he kissed the head tenderly. Then, he opened his jaw and took Cal into his mouth.

Cal moaned in response to the erogenous sensations resulting from Jacob's oral stimulation. He grasped the headboard of the bed and arched his back as Jacob continued to fondle his groin with his tongue and lips. Feeling relaxed and comfortable, Cal began enjoying this intimate moment with his date.

"Um, I'm getting close," Cal warned as the arousing stimulation in his groin escalated. Jacob relinquished his erection.

"Huh?" he asked.

"I'm getting close," Cal repeated.

"Good," Jacob replied with a playful smile. He massaged Cal's chest and began kissing his lips before moving his way back down to his waist.

Jacob once again took Cal into his mouth and ran his tongue along the rim, accompanied by Cal's moans of enjoyment. After several moments, a warm, tingling sensation formed at the base of his groin, and he arched his back as he ejaculated. Jacob's mouth remained on his erection, welcoming the orgasm. Cal sighed in gratification as he released the last spurts of semen, but his pleasure was temporary, and a shadow of guilt plagued the bedroom. Despite his supposed feelings for Jacob, Cal felt somewhat shameful for allowing that to happen on their second date. Even worse, he now wished it was Andrew who had gone down on him, his thoughts interfering with his intimate moment with Jacob.

Jacob lifted his head and smiled; despite Cal's guilt and unease, he forced himself to smile back. Jacob kissed his mouth and then cuddled him in his arms as he closed his eyes. Cal felt disgusted with himself as Jacob held him and wished to be anywhere else besides that bedroom.

"You're such a great guy," Jacob stated as he kissed him on the cheek.

"Thanks," Cal replied in a flat tone of voice, as his shame increased exponentially.

The two lay on the bed cuddling, Jacob completely content and restful while Cal was screaming inside, frustrated at himself and his irrational emotions. After a while, Cal made the move to leave.

"It's getting late. I better go."

"Aw, I wish you could stay," Jacob toyed.

"I wish I could too," Cal lied.

"Well, I'll walk you out." The two men dressed and then left the apartment in silence.

"I'm glad we could hang out again," Jacob smiled as they reached Cal's car.

"Yeah, me too," he responded.

"Hopefully, I'll get to see you again soon."

"Yeah, for sure," Cal replied with a fake grin as Jacob leaned in to kiss him. His lips were warm, tender, and passionate, yet Cal could only continue to taste self-disgust. After several moments, the two broke apart, and Cal drove off into the night.

He arrived home feeling upset and ashamed, and collapsed on his bed. He was exhausted, yet he could not put his thoughts to rest as he reflected on his date with Jacob. Cal was no prude, but he regretted what had occurred since it made him feel sleazy. Even worse, he began to miss Andrew.

Bitter tears welled in Cal's eyes. Feeling like he was leading Jacob on, wishing he was with Andrew, and focusing on how unfulfilled he was in life, Cal could not hold back his sorrow any longer. He let the salty tears stream down his cheeks and stain his pillowcase. After several minutes of silent sobs, Cal's damp eyes grew heavy with exhaustion, and he fell asleep shortly after.

Chapter Nine

Three and a half years earlier

Weeks rolled by without Cal ever hearing a word from Andrew. He was miserable, though he tried to convince himself that their estrangement was for the best. To no one's surprise, Cal had been offered the job—which he was unwilling to accept—and he was slated to move to his new apartment the day after graduation. His transition into adulthood was inevitable.

Despite what seemed to be a promising start to his postgrad life, Cal struggled to get through the remaining days of his semester. Each dreary day seemed to grow more and more gray as autumn dragged on. Cal felt as though he were an empty vessel, existing through each day instead of actually living. He was reminded that he was still alive only by the aching of his heart and the stinging of his eyes as he fought to hold back tears of sorrow at night.

After he had withdrawn from almost all social activities for two weeks, Cal's friends managed to convince him to go out to the bars with them on Halloween. Dressed in a *Clark Kent* costume and a fake smile, Cal forced himself to leave the comfort of his sullen isolation in an attempt to enjoy the company of his friends.

They arrived at the first bar around ten thirty, had a couple of drinks, and took a few pictures. However, Cal was ready to go home before midnight and left by himself. A light drizzle fell on the chilly October evening as Cal trudged back to his apartment, staring down at his sneakers and weaving through cheery, costumed crowds. He thought it was ironic that he was dressed as a superhero, yet he felt so weak. Even though he had tried to have fun, Cal couldn't ignore the ache in his chest; everything seemed so dull and pointless.

Two days later, while sulking in his apartment, Cal received a text from Andrew:

> *Hey I saw your Halloween pics on Facebook. You make a damn sexy superman.*

> *Ha ha thanks.*

Cal wondered what on earth Andrew could possibly want.

> *I know I said I didn't think we should see each other but what if I said I take it back?*

That's funny, I don't remember you ever saying that explicitly. All you did was give me a half-assed apology saying you were backing off, Cal recalled. Nevertheless, Andrew's sudden message had tugged at his heart.

> *I got the job though and I graduate in a little over a month. What happens then?*

> *Let's cross that bridge when we get there. Like you said, a lot can happen between now and then.*

Cal knew he shouldn't take the bait. He knew he shouldn't go out with Andrew again. He knew he would only be left broken, but that didn't matter because Cal couldn't resist Andrew.

The two made plans to have dinner at a local restaurant that upcoming Friday. Although Cal was eager to once again be in Andrew's presence and experience his seductive touch once more, his heart still ached from his confusion. Andrew said they would figure out their situation once December grew nearer, but the fact of the matter was that Cal would be leaving soon. So what was going to happen to their relationship? Was what they had even considered a relationship? Time was running out.

Despite this, Cal was still excited while preparing for their date. He pulled up to Andrew's apartment and waited impatiently as his heart thudded. Cal gazed out through his windshield and stared at the courtyard adjacent to the row of brick-clad apartments. Several skinny trees were barren and their now dead leaves had littered the pale grass. The drab scenery was so different compared to the last time Cal had been there in mid-October.

Once Andrew stepped out of his apartment and got into Cal's car, they drove to the restaurant. As they conversed over dinner, Cal was amazed by how it was always so easy for them to pick up where they'd left off. He wondered if only he was upset by their periods of silence, or if Andrew was also pretending that he was not bothered by their estrangement.

After dinner, the two went back to Cal's apartment, and as before, they were soon locked in a passionate embrace on the bed. Andrew's touch was intoxicating, and Cal was addicted. He knew Andrew's kiss would leave him with false hope and heartache, but he couldn't deny it. Cal needed his fix, and in those moments with Andrew, the temporary pleasure compensated for the pain that always lingered after their dates.

Andrew slipped Cal out of his shirt and then lay him on his back. He settled himself next to him before running his hand through Cal's chest hair. His hand lingered there for a moment before it slid tantalizingly down Cal's torso and rested on his waist. Without hesitation, Andrew slid his hand into Cal's pants and began caressing him.

"Is this okay?" he whispered.

"Yeah," Cal breathed before he helped Andrew out of his shirt.

Andrew kissed his neck for a moment before he began stroking Cal's erection. Cal curled his toes as he groaned in pleasure and then reached for Andrew.

This was all new to Cal. He had never been touched like this, nor had he ever touched someone back to that extent. Though pleasurable, it was a foreign experience that was somewhat uncomfortable to Cal for fear of not performing to Andrew's expectations. Still, Cal grasped his crush's bulge and ran his hand up and down his shaft.

The two lovers lay shirtless on their backs, side by side, and synchronized their hand movements, working to get each other off. In what seemed like no time at all, Andrew came. The warm ejaculate dribbled out onto his hand as the sticky fluid spurted from Andrew's erection, which coated his smooth chest and stomach. Andrew took in a deep breath and sighed in relaxation before turning his attention back to Cal's groin.

Andrew continued attempting to get Cal off, while he willed himself to climax. The stimulating touch of Andrew's hand was arousing and yet Cal struggled to achieve an orgasm since there was too much on his mind. What was going to happen tomorrow between him and

Andrew? Would Andrew be waking up next to him? Would he be Cal's boyfriend after this? Would he and Andrew slip back into a period of familiar silence? What was going to happen next month when Cal graduates?

These worries prevented him from enjoying the moment, and his erection soon began to go soft.

"Damn, dude, are you getting close?" Andrew wondered. "My arm is starting to get sore."

Several unsuccessful minutes passed before Andrew relinquished his grip on Cal's flaccid penis. Cal was embarrassed by the fact that he was unable to come and concerned about what would happen after that night, but he kept these troubles to himself as he cuddled and kissed Andrew briefly.

After a short time, Andrew rolled off the bed and walked over to the kitchen so he could grab some paper towels to wipe the dried ejaculate off his stomach. Once he had cleaned himself off, he asked Cal to take him home, claiming he had to attend a twenty-first birthday party that night and Cal obliged.

He returned to his apartment after dropping Andrew off at only nine thirty, feeling lonely and dejected. What happened between them that night was no light matter—at least not to Cal. However, Andrew had been so nonchalant about the situation and then left to go to a party. Why would he have agreed to a date if he was going to leave early? Did Andrew possess any deeper feelings for Cal, or was he merely a convenience?

Regardless, Cal held his head high and kept his spirits lifted. He and Andrew continued to converse for several days afterward, leading him to believe they still had a chance. However, Andrew soon began to back off until any communication the two had petered out, leaving Cal vulnerable and upset.

When he went home for Thanksgiving break, he ached from faking a pleasant demeanor around his family. Cal hadn't told them about Andrew, nor would he ever. What was the point? It's not as if they were going to be together. Despite his heartbreak, Cal lied to himself and his family and recited a rehearsed line—that he was excited to uproot from the foundation he had built in college and start over in isolation for a job.

Chapter Ten

"Ow, ow. Look at you, stud," Sophie teased as Cal got into her car. The two had made plans to go out to the mall that afternoon to complete their Christmas shopping. "It's only been a week since I've seen you, and already you have whiskers—and a new haircut."

"Ha ha, yeah. What do you think?" Cal asked while he fastened his seat belt.

"I like it a lot," she complimented as she pulled out of the parking lot and drove toward the mall.

"Thanks."

"For real, you look hot."

"That's good, 'cause I feel like shit," he admitted.

"Why?" Sophie questioned.

"Well, I hung out with Jacob earlier this week."

"Good, I'm glad you went out with him again. How did it go?"

"Fine. Actually, it went pretty well—at first," Cal said. "We went to the movies and...it was nice. We held hands, and I was comfortable with him. And happy. I think I was starting to like him."

"That's great," she exclaimed. "So, why are you feeling shitty?"

"Like I said, I was starting to like him, and he invited me over to his place for a drink. And then we..."

"Then you what?" Sophie prodded, detecting Cal's hesitation.

"Um—"

"Come on, Cal. We've known each other forever. There's not much you can say that'll phase me."

"Okay. We kinda hooked up."

"Like hooked up or *hooked up*?"

"He gave me a blowjob."

"How was it?"

"It was...okay," Cal replied.

"What's the problem? Did he use too much teeth or something?" Sophie wondered, unsure of what Cal's issue was.

"No, it's nothing Jacob did," he clarified. "I started thinking about Andrew toward the end of it. And afterward, I felt dirty almost. Like I was screwing over Jacob by letting him blow me when I wasn't even that into it."

Sophie remained silent and stared ahead at the road, but Cal saw her bite her lip.

"What?" he questioned.

"Please don't get mad at me for saying this, but this is what you do?"

"Do you think I'm some kind of man whore? I've only been with—"

"No, I don't think that at all. I know you rarely hook up. What I'm saying is, every time you've dated a guy in the past that you could've actually liked, you get cold feet. If it starts feeling serious, you find some reason not to like him."

"I know," Cal admitted. "But I'm not sure why I do that."

"That's not true. We both know why you do that."

"Because of Andrew," he muttered.

"Because of Andrew," Sophie repeated. "I think you might be scared to let yourself like someone more than him. It almost seems like you're scared of commitment and abandonment."

"I'm not scared of commitment. I'm scared of committing myself to the wrong person...again," Cal reasoned. "And it's not that I'm scared of liking someone more than Andrew. I'm over him. I just get scared that I won't do better than him."

"I've seen pictures of him online; you've dated guys better than him."

"They seem better than him on paper, but nothing ever feels right. I never get that feeling I had with him," Cal sighed. "And then I get scared that I'm gonna wake up one day, married to some guy. We'll have a great house and amazing careers and a family..."

"That sounds nice," Sophie commented.

"It does," he agreed. "Except I won't be happy; not completely anyway. Yeah, I'll think it seems like a great life, and sure, I'll get along with my husband, but I'm scared I won't fully love him. It's like there's some part of me that's still invested in Andrew, and I'll always wonder what would've happened if I didn't take that stupid job."

"Hey, listen to me. You've got to let go of the past. You can't wonder what could've happened; focus on what *did* happen," she urged. "Yes, you left, but he could've had four months with you before you moved. He could've said something to you before you left. But he *didn't.*

"I'm sorry, I don't want to be mean, but you've got to look at what he did to you. And, yeah, you had some struggles when you moved, but look at everything you did for yourself since then. You don't need him. And honestly, even if you did stay, he probably would've screwed you over, and then you might've been kicking yourself in the ass about not taking that job."

"I know. I know. And I'm over him and coming to peace with the past...or at least I was. Then he showed up at my parents' door with my sister," Cal muttered. "It's like whenever I feel like I've moved on from that situation, something happens that pulls me back in."

"I really hate him," Sophie said.

"I do too. But I still want him."

"Is that what all this is about?" she inquired as she gestured toward Cal. "The new haircut and clothes? Is all this to show up Andrew?"

Cal remained silent in his seat and gazed out the window.

"I know I said you should make him regret the past, but be careful, okay?" Sophie warned. "I get that you want to impress him and be your best, but you need to take care of yourself. You still have feelings for him, for whatever reason, and I don't want to see you get hurt again. Promise me you'll be careful."

"Sophie, I'm twenty-five years old—"

"Yes, I know you are. And I know it's been a few years, but that doesn't make Andrew any less of a fuckboy. So promise me."

"Fine, I promise," Cal said as he rolled his eyes.

"Good," Sophie replied. The two remained quiet as Sophie pulled into the bustling parking lot at the mall. As the car came to a stop, she broke the silence. "By the way, if your offer still stands, I'd love to join you and your family for Christmas."

"Of course it still stands. I'll let my mom know."

"Okay, good," Sophie said as they got out of the car and headed toward the mall. "So, are you gonna see Jacob again?"

"I don't know," Cal sighed. "He texted me this morning, but I haven't answered yet."

"Well, I think you should go out with him again, but don't hook up like that again," she instructed. "You seemed to have had feelings for him the other night. I think you just need to get to know him a little better."

"Yeah, you're probably right."

The two friends spent several hours in the crowded mall to finalize their Christmas shopping. By the end of the day, they were exhausted but relieved to have purchased a gift for everyone on their lists. Cal, who was now on a strict budget after buying his new car, was pleased he had not spent more than the amount of money he had allotted for gifts.

He and Sophie were famished by the time they left the mall, and decided to stop at a sushi restaurant for dinner. Cal arrived home just after seven, though it seemed much later due to the early evening darkness that seemed to fall sooner and sooner each night. Exhausted from his day out with Sophie, Cal changed into his pajamas and then began packing in preparation for his weeklong Christmas "vacation" with his family and Andrew.

God, help me get through this week, he thought as he folded a dress shirt and placed it in his suitcase. When his phone buzzed in his pocket, he pulled it out and found a welcome distraction—Jacob was calling.

"Hello?" Cal answered as he walked to the closet to retrieve a black vest.

"Hey, I'm surprised you picked up," Jacob said lightly.

"Yeah, I'm sorry. The past couple days have been pretty busy for me."

"No worries. You seemed kind of quiet after Tuesday night. I wanted to make sure I didn't scare you off."

"No, not at all," Cal lied.

"Okay, good," he replied. "I know I texted you this already, but I just wanted to say I hope I didn't make you feel uncomfortable on Tuesday."

"No, I was fine with everything. I mean, I usually don't go that far on a second date, so I don't want you to think I'm looking for a hookup."

"Good, and I don't want you to think I'm looking for a hookup either. I'm relationship oriented."

"Okay, cool," Cal said before an awkward pause settled over them.

"Well, while I have you here, would you want to hang out tomorrow night?" Jacob asked.

"I can't tomorrow night because I'll be heading over to my parents' at six."

"Oh, okay." Cal felt a tinge of guilt hearing the disappointment in Jacob's voice.

"But I'll be free all day besides that," he offered. "I'm not sure what your schedule is like for tomorrow."

"Things have been pretty quiet at work, so I think I should be able to get away with a long lunch," Jacob replied.

"Great."

"There's a really great Mediterranean place right around the corner from my office. How about we meet there at twelve thirty?"

"Sounds good."

"All right, cool. I'll text you the address. Have a good night, handsome."

"Thanks, you too," Cal said. As he hung up, he was surprised to find a smile on his face, but he welcomed it. While he remained unsure about Jacob, he definitely made Cal feel good. He probably did like Jacob so he needed to make sure he wouldn't let Andrew get in his head and ruin this for him.

The next morning, Cal woke at his regular time and started his day with a workout. Afterward, he finished packing up a few last minute items and then showered. Shortly before noon, Cal left his apartment and drove over to the restaurant where he was supposed to meet Jacob. When he walked inside, Cal scanned the restaurant. He found Jacob seated at a booth nearby, which caused excited butterflies to form in his stomach.

See, you do like him, he assured himself as he walked over to Jacob. The two men smiled and gave each other a friendly hug before they sat and eyed their menus.

They spent their lunch conversing about various topics, including what Jacob had been doing at work over the past week. They discussed their individual holiday plans as well, and Cal informed Jacob he was going to be spending the week with his family. The food was delicious and the conversation was good, but soon Cal's thoughts drifted to his week ahead with Andrew, which he both dreaded and looked forward to. He tried not to let these thoughts preoccupy his mind and put on a poker face, but Jacob seemed to notice.

"Are you okay?" he asked.

"What?" Cal replied as he processed Jacob's question that had caught him off guard. "Oh, yeah. I'm fine."

"You're a bad liar," Jacob said with a lighthearted chuckle.

"No really, I'm okay," he said, though his flushed face said otherwise. He didn't want to bring up his dating history while he was hanging out with Jacob.

"If it's something you want to talk about, you can tell me." Cal peered into Jacob's gentle, light-blue eyes, and something about them made him feel so comfortable.

"Okay," Cal replied. "Well, you know how I said that my family is having Christmas at my parents' house?"

"Yeah."

"Well, my sister is bringing her boyfriend...and her boyfriend is my ex."

"Um, okay. What—?"

"Andrew—my ex...well, my sister's boyfriend—I never told my family about him."

"Um, was it...serious?" Jacob asked, careful not to be too intrusive. "Sorry, I hope you don't mind me asking that."

"It's fine. And in hindsight, it wasn't serious, but it felt serious to me. He screwed me over, so seeing him again is obviously a little...*unsettling*."

"Well," Jacob began after a brief pause, "he's an idiot for letting you get away."

Cal laughed.

"I mean it, he's an idiot. But I'm sure that still doesn't make it any easier for you."

"It certainly doesn't," Cal confirmed.

"Well, if you need to escape from the chaos at your parents' house or just need to vent, feel free to let me know," he offered with a soothing smile.

"Thank you."

Cal and Jacob eased off the topic of Andrew and resumed conversing over lunch. When they both finished their meals, Cal paid for them and the two men left the restaurant together. Jacob walked Cal to his car and— after checking to make sure they were out of sight—kissed him. His gentle lips communicated a sense of comfort, and for a moment Cal felt safe while the holiday stressors seemed to dissipate. Feeling his guard lower, Cal grasped Jacob's coat lapels, and their kiss deepened. His date reciprocated by wrapping his arms around Cal's slender waist when a nearby car horn reminded them that the two were in public. They broke apart abruptly, and Jacob gave him a final tender peck before they parted ways.

Cal drove home feeling a bit giddy, with his heart beating in his chest. He definitely had a connection with Jacob and wanted to see where it could lead. He reminded himself to hold onto that feeling, to get him through the upcoming holiday.

Cal arrived at his apartment just after two and took his packed bags out to his car. Once it was loaded, he laid the Christmas gifts he had purchased on his kitchen table and began wrapping them as the minutes ticked closer and closer to six.

At five thirty, Cal could not procrastinate any longer, and he determined that he would need to leave in a few minutes to arrive at his parents' house on time. He decided to change into some of the new clothes he had bought a few days earlier and he threw on a pair of dark-washed jeans, stylish winter boots, and a white thermal shirt that complemented his toned body. Then, Cal threw on his coat, carried the wrapped gifts out to his car, and left his apartment.

Cal arrived at his parents' home just after six and saw what he assumed to be Andrew's car already parked in the driveway. Cal's body trembled a bit as he pulled his keys out of the ignition, and he drew a deep breath.

You'll be fine, Cal reassured himself as he retrieved his luggage and the wrapped gifts from the trunk of his car. He knew he would be seeing Andrew and had spent the last week preparing for this moment. Sure, it would sting to see his ex again, but Cal couldn't let that affect him. He had to prove to Andrew how much better off he was without him—even if Cal doubted that himself.

"Gotta fake it till you make it," Cal muttered aloud before he opened the front door and stepped into the toasty home.

"Hello?" his mother's voice echoed from the kitchen, over the clinking of dishes. "That better be my son walking through the door."

"It is," Cal responded as he removed his coat and set his things off to the side.

"You're late," Mrs. Adams stated, still unseen in the kitchen.

"I know. I'm sorry," he apologized as he walked into the kitchen and was bombarded by an array of scrumptious aromas. His mother was bent over in front of the oven, tending to dinner.

"Oh my God! Look at you!" she exclaimed when she stood up and faced Cal. "You look great!"

"Thanks," he chuckled lightly.

"New hair. And, oh, you're growing your beard back," Mrs. Adams remarked and pinched Cal's cheek before giving him a maternal peck.

"Hey, Cal," his father called from the staircase, "I saw that new car in the driveway from the window upstairs—"

"New car?" his mother wondered.

"Is that yours?" Mr. Adams asked.

"You bought a new car?" she questioned.

"Yeah," Cal replied to both of his parents.

"Nice!" his father exclaimed. "What year is it?"

"You bought a new car?" Mrs. Adams repeated. "What? Are you having a quarter-life crisis?"

"It's only a year old. And I told you my car died on me last week."

"Yeah, but you didn't say you got a new car."

"Well, what was I supposed to do? Drive around with a rental?"

"I didn't say that, but your car only died a week ago. That's awfully fast to—"

"What's the engine like?" his father called, now staring at the car from the front door.

"It's really nice, Dad. Want to take it for a ride later?" Cal offered. Mr. Adams, who rarely ever splurged on purchases, always received a thrill of excitement whenever a neighbor or family friend bought a new car.

"Yeah!"

"All right, well not now," Mrs. Adams replied. "It's almost time for dinner. Claire and Andrew are waiting in the dining room."

"I'm gonna put my bags in the guest room," Cal stated and left the kitchen, while his mother fiddled with a pot on the stove. He traipsed up the stairs and deposited his luggage in the guest room before he sank onto the bed. To his surprise, Cal's anxiety had almost completely subsided. Instead, he was emotionally exhausted from keeping up this charade. Nevertheless, he refused to appear vulnerable to Andrew, so Cal mustered up all the positivity he could find deep within himself and headed downstairs into the dining room.

"Cal!" Claire called out an excited greeting, as she leapt up from her chair and hugged him. "I love the haircut...and the scruff."

"Thanks," he replied with a smile and then turned toward Andrew. A slight pang of desire welled up inside Cal, but he silenced it as he offered his ex a hug. "Hey, Andrew. Great to see you again!"

"Uh, yeah. You too," he replied. Andrew seemed to have been thrown off by Cal's composed, sociable demeanor compared to the last time they had seen each other, but he recovered as Mrs. Adams bustled into the dining room with a sizzling roast and began to serve dinner. Cal took his seat at the table, but not before he noticed Andrew quickly eye him up and down, observing—and perhaps lusting for—this new and improved version of himself.

Per usual, Mrs. Adams had outdone herself and cooked up a delectable meal. Cal was pleased to discover that unlike their previous family dinner, this one went much smoother. The conversation had remained pleasant and Cal avoided any awkward interjections. Maybe he could fake his way through this week.

After dessert—a mouthwatering tiramisu—Claire volunteered to wash the dishes, despite their mother's protests. Cal sat at the table with his parents and Andrew, and the group sipped their coffee while chattering away about the upcoming holidays. However, Cal's courage soon ebbed as he made eye contact with Andrew, so he excused himself to assist Claire.

"Hey," she greeted him as he entered the kitchen, carrying in the last few dirty plates with him.

"I thought I'd lend a hand," he offered.

"Great, thanks."

As the siblings scrubbed away at the scraps of food stuck on the dinner plates, they discussed their current endeavors regarding school and work. As their conversation subsided, Claire bit her lip.

"Um, can I ask you something?"

"Sure, what's up?" Cal inquired.

"I'm not quite sure how to ask this," she began, "but do you like Andrew?"

"What—?"

"Last time he was here, things seemed a little *awkward*...and you seemed a little dismissive of him."

"Oh. Uh, yeah, I like him," Cal assured as he swallowed hard. "He seems like a great guy."

"Really?"

"Yeah!"

"Okay, good," Claire breathed in relief as she placed a serving tray in the dishwasher, "because your opinion really matters to me, and I like him. *A lot.*"

"Oh, nice," Cal replied, and for a moment he felt weakened despite the confident exterior he had been attempting to display that evening. "Are things pretty serious between you two?"

"Yeah," she beamed, as if she was a young schoolgirl experiencing her first innocent crush. "I've been in relationships before, but I've never felt like this. I don't know what it is, but there's just something about him."

"I know exactly what you mean," he said.

"So, what about you?" Claire probed, as she sensed her brother's minor dismay. "Are you seeing anyone?"

"You know me, Claire. I'm always seeing someone," he answered with a slight chuckle.

"Well, are you seeing anyone worthwhile?" she pressed.

"I'm not sure yet," Cal said. With Jacob in mind, he wanted to say yes, but Andrew had begun to creep into his thoughts again. "I'll be sure to let you know when I figure it out."

"There are my wonderful kiddies. Thank you so much for doing the dishes," Mrs. Adams said as she walked into the kitchen with a glass of wine—her third that night—in hand.

"Mom, it was nothing," Claire dismissed.

"Well, I appreciate it," their mother replied. "Oh, you two look so cute standing there together. Let me take a picture."

"Ugh come on, Mom." Cal said.

"Oh, would you just shut up and humor your mother," she retorted as she pulled her cell phone from her bag. "Okay, move a little closer together and smile."

Cal put his arm around Claire and the two smiled while their mother fidgeted with the phone's camera.

"Oh shit. How do I turn on the flash? Oh, wait. There we go. Okay, ready? Smile," she instructed as she snapped the picture and examined it. "Oh, would you look at that. I really do have gorgeous children. Let me show your father. Hey, Todd, look at this."

Cal and Claire rolled their eyes in unison and attempted to stifle their laughter as they finished washing the last of the dishes.

Later that night, after everyone had gone to bed, Cal remained downstairs to relax and ruminate in silent tranquility. He went over to the liquor cabinet and poured himself a whiskey—his father's favorite—before he retired to the family room. Cal settled himself on the couch in front of the lit fireplace and was quite cozy dressed in his lounge pants and hoodie. He gazed into the gentle flames as he sipped his drink.

The night had gone better than Cal expected, though his defense had worn a bit thin toward the end of the evening. Andrew had definitely been eyeing him up throughout dinner, which did little to ease his anxiety. Cal had succeeded in showing his ex what he had missed out on. However, that no longer seemed to be enough for Cal. He almost wanted a second chance with Andrew, though he knew he was being irrational and hurried to force his lustful thoughts out of his head.

Cal pulled his phone from his pocket, to distract him from these thoughts. He opened his messages and smiled as he read through his conversation with Jacob from that day. He was a gentleman with a good sense of humor, and treated Cal well—something he was seldom used to. More importantly, Jacob seemed invested in him and interested in getting to know him more.

Cal had begun to accept that he had feelings for Jacob, and he tried to focus on that so as not to let himself fall for Andrew again. This was the first time in a long time he had a rational crush where there were no red flags, no excuses for poor behavior, and no faked feelings. This had the potential to become something real, and Cal didn't want to risk losing that.

His attention was diverted from the crackling fire as a creak resonated from the adjacent staircase.

"Hey," his father said as he entered the family room. "I thought I heard someone down here."

"I'm just having a nightcap," Cal informed him as he tilted his glass.

"Mind if I join you?" Mr. Adams asked.

"Not at all," he replied as his father poured himself a whiskey before taking a seat on a nearby reclining chair.

"Oh, that's good," he said after sipping his drink. "I feel like I didn't get a chance to talk with you at dinner. Your mother tends to dominate the conversation."

Cal laughed.

"How are things with you?"

"Can't complain," he replied before taking a swig of whiskey. "The gym's still closed, so that sucks."

"Do they have any idea when it's going to reopen yet?"

"Not yet. It's nice having some time off from work, but I've been feeling kind of stir crazy lately."

"Is that why you bought a new car?"

"Dad, no. My car died and it was time for an upgrade. And I got it for a pretty good deal."

"Good, so you're not going through some quarter-life crisis?" Mr. Adams teased.

"Not yet," Cal chuckled.

"Glad to hear. I'd hate to see you go through a life crisis at such a young age, since you have a lot of great things going for you."

Cal scoffed at his father's remark.

"No, I'm being serious, Cal. You've got an education and a good job. You're responsible with your finances, and you've got your health," Mr. Adams commented.

"Well, that's not everything," Cal said to himself before sipping his drink. His father eyed him and took a quick glug of his own beverage.

"Cal, can I ask you something?"

"What?"

"How come you never bring anyone around?" he wondered.

"What?" Cal repeated as he choked on his whiskey, having been caught off guard by his father's question. His palms grew clammy around his almost empty glass as he realized what his father was getting at.

"You're twenty-five years old and a good-looking guy, so I'm assuming you date," Mr. Adams remarked. "So how come you never bring anyone around? Your mother and I would be happy to meet whoever you're dating."

"Who says I'm dating anyone? Maybe I'm a loner."

"Well, if you were dating someone..."

"Dad, it's not that simple."

"Why not?"

"Because, it's just not! Okay?" Cal retorted in an unintentionally raised voice.

His father took the cue that Cal no longer wanted to speak about the topic and grew quiet, though he appeared dejected.

Cal eyed his father and felt a bit guilty. Though he had always felt uncomfortable talking about his dating life with his parents, perhaps he was being somewhat selfish by keeping that from them. Maybe they did want to know from time to time if he was seeing anyone. Cal emptied his glass, sighed, and then spoke.

"I do date, Dad, but it's never anything serious. I wish it got to the point where I was in a serious enough relationship to bring someone around...but..."

"But what?" he father inquired.

"But," Cal said before biting his lip. He wasn't at all drunk; he was barely even tipsy. However, as uneasy as he was, he still had the urge to divulge a secret to his father—a secret that only Sophie knew. "Okay, the truth is I got hurt...bad. About three years ago, right around the time I was graduating. I really liked this...*guy* who acted like...like *he* really liked me, but then he would pull away. I always blamed myself for it and thought it was because of the timing.

"But I realized he was just a player. Or at least I thought he was. I don't know, but stuff has happened somewhat recently with that situation, so now I don't know what to think. Anyway, I'm not sure if I ever got over it. And that's why I've never had a serious relationship."

Though he was somewhat embarrassed, Cal was relieved to have disclosed this information to his father, after years of building walls to seal off his dating history from his family. Still, he avoided eye contact and stared into his empty glass as he waited for Mr. Adams to speak.

"Well," his father began and set down his drink, "I hate to sound cliché, but everything has a way of working out in the end, and if it wasn't meant to be, it wasn't meant to be."

"Yeah, you're right," Cal concurred.

"And honestly, this guy sounds like trash," he continued. "I wouldn't want a guy like that around you. I wouldn't want a guy like that around Claire. You guys deserve better."

"I know."

"Don't worry, you'll find it when you least expect it," Mr. Adams assured him. "Do you see the way Claire and Andrew look at each other? *That* is love. And you'll find that someday."

"Do you think they're actually in love?"

"Oh, I know it," his father replied with a curious twinkle in his eyes.

"Can we talk about something else?" Cal asked as his stomach churned uneasily at his father's comments.

"Sure," he replied and finished his whiskey. "So when are you gonna let me drive your car?"

Cal laughed. He and his father poured themselves another drink and continued to chat for a while until the clock's chime interrupted them at midnight. Mr. Adams determined it was time for him to turn in for the night. He swallowed the last mouthful of liquor and then rose from the couch. As he walked past Cal, he placed a hand upon his son's shoulder.

"Love you, bud," he said, giving him a reassuring squeeze.

"Love you too, Dad." Cal's father retreated upstairs and left him alone to finish his drink in front of the dimming fireplace. As he sipped the last of his whiskey, Cal reflected on his father's words.

Mr. Adams had seemed to believe what Claire and Andrew had was love—something that had not been there between Cal and Andrew. Perhaps he had been oblivious to the connection between his sister and his ex since he was so caught up in showing himself off to Andrew.

I've never felt like this before. I don't know what it is, but there's just something about him.

Cal recalled Claire's blissful expression as she gushed over Andrew earlier. His sister was in love, and he had been blind to this until now. Maybe he should let go of his infatuation with Andrew. No, he *had* to let go of his infatuation with Andrew. It wasn't fair for Cal to stand in the way of Claire's happiness. This could be true love, something that probably would have never flourished between Cal and Andrew—even if he had stayed.

Besides, it appeared as if there was potential with Jacob. Mr. Adams was right: everything has a way of working out in the end. Maybe this could be the closure Cal needed. He could move on and find his own happiness—maybe with Jacob.

Feeling somewhat at ease, Cal finished his drink and grew drowsy. He extinguished the last of the embers in the fireplace and then prepared for bed. As he climbed under the toasty covers, Cal repeated his father's words.

Everything has a way of working out in the end.

The next morning, Cal awoke before nine and still felt rather content from his conversation with his father. After gazing out the window and discovering it was a clear, sunny morning, he decided to go for a leisurely run to further ease his mind. Cal changed into his running shorts and a tight tank top and grabbed his zip-up athletic hoodie before heading downstairs into the kitchen for a light breakfast.

"Good morning, sweetie," his mother greeted as she fried some eggs in a sizzling pan. Claire and Andrew were seated at the kitchen table with mugs of steaming coffee.

"Morning," Cal replied.

"You want some eggs?" Mrs. Adams asked.

"No thanks, I'm getting ready to go for a run," he informed her as he grabbed a cup of plain Greek yogurt from the fridge.

"Oh, mind if we come with you?" Claire inquired as she set down her coffee.

"Um—"

"I didn't bring any running clothes," Andrew admitted, with a concerned expression.

"And he probably doesn't have the right shoes," Cal added.

"Your father has a bunch of extra sneakers," Mrs. Adams laughed as she flipped the eggs. "He buys a new pair every spring, convinced that he's going to run the community half marathon in the summer. You can borrow a pair of his, Andrew."

"And I'm sure Cal has an extra pair of shorts, right?" Claire wondered.

"I'm not sure," Andrew began.

"Oh come on, it'll be fun. It's good exercise," she insisted.

"I'll grab you a pair of shorts," Cal said flatly since he knew it was no use arguing with his persistent sister. "It'll be *so* much fun."

"Come on, Andrew," their mother said as she swept him out of the kitchen. "Let's find you a pair of shoes that fit."

"Does he even run?" Cal questioned his sister, once they were alone in the kitchen.

"Sometimes he runs with me. He's been trying to get into it," Claire explained before lowering her voice. "I want you guys to hang out and get to know each other."

Oh believe me, we know each other plenty well. Still, he wanted to respect his sister's wishes and happiness. Besides, this was a new start for Cal. He was happy getting to know Jacob, and Claire was happy with Andrew. Everything would be fine. Everybody was happy. "Fine, I'll grab him a pair of shorts."

Cal went to his room and retrieved a spare, looser-fitting pair of basketball shorts since there was a size difference between the two men. Once everyone had changed into their running attire and Andrew had found a pair of shoes that fit, the trio stepped outside. Despite the sunny, clear sky, it was still rather chilly out, and Cal zipped his hoodie up to protect himself from the wind.

"Let's stretch real quick," he instructed.

"Careful, don't rip your pants," Claire teased Andrew as he bent over to stretch his calves. Despite being a looser fit on Cal, the basketball shorts were still a smidge too small on Andrew—particularly around his buttocks. Cal couldn't help but stare for a moment and broke his gaze before Claire or Andrew noticed.

"Shut up," he laughed as he stood up. "I told you I'm working on getting back into shape."

After they had all stretched, the group took off on an easy jog through the snow-covered neighborhood. The three ran side by side for the first few minutes until Andrew fell a bit behind. Cal and Claire continued in stride together and chatted with ease, despite their slight panting. After about a mile or so, Claire glanced back behind her to assess how far ahead of Andrew they were.

"So much for you guys getting to know each other," she chuckled. "Go on ahead. I'll wait for Andrew."

"You sure?"

"Yeah. I know I'm slowing you down anyway," Claire laughed.

With his sister's permission, Cal took off at his usual pace. He breathed the crisp air in deeply and exhaled as he extended his legs and sprinted several yards ahead of Claire and Andrew. The bitter gusts slapped his face mercilessly and his leg muscled burnt hot with exertion, but Cal was invigorated. With each step, he was eliminating all the stress, anxiety, and worry from his body.

"Cal!" his sister's voice echoed throughout the tranquil, winter morning. He glanced behind him and saw Andrew seated at the curb with Claire standing over him. Cal spun around and jogged over to them.

"What's wrong?" he questioned; as he approached he could see that Claire appeared concerned.

"It's his leg," she informed with a tinge of worry in her voice.

"I probably just pulled a muscle," Andrew shrugged with a slight wince as he rubbed his aching thigh.

"What do you think?" Claire asked her brother.

"What do you mean?" Cal wondered.

"Is his leg okay?"

"I'm not a doctor," he exclaimed.

"But you work at a gym."

"Yeah, but I went to school for business management."

"But you're taking those personal training courses," Claire countered. "Don't they teach you about treating basic sport-related injuries?"

"Yeah, but I haven't gotten certified yet," Cal retorted.

"Would you please take a look at his leg?"

"Fine," he replied grudgingly before turning toward Andrew. "Where, specifically, does it hurt?"

"A little above my knee," he answered. Cal knelt next to him and placed a hand on Andrew's meaty thigh.

"All right," he began, without making eye contact with his ex. "I'm gonna place pressure on it. Tell me when it hurts."

"Okay," Andrew said. Cal squeezed various spots on his thigh until Andrew winced. "Ow, right there."

"Yeah," he said as he detected a firm lump. "I can feel a knot there. Your muscles were probably tight from the cold."

Cal began to massage Andrew's thigh to work it out. Bittersweet memories of driving around with his hand on Andrew's leg began replaying in his mind. Cal's face flushed as he peered up at his ex. Damn, something about his dark-brown eyes was so inviting. For a moment, the two gazed at each other while Cal continued to massage the muscle.

"How does it feel?" Claire asked sounding concerned.

"It feels good," Cal blurted out in a low voice. When he realized what he had said, he broke eye contact and stood. "I mean, it feels like the muscle is relaxed. Can you walk?"

"Yeah," Andrew responded as he got to his feet. "Um, thanks."

"Don't mention it."

Andrew stretched out his leg, and then the group walked back home. Claire chattered away, oblivious to the awkwardness of Cal's thigh massage. He and Andrew, however, remained silent and gazed ahead to avoid eye contact for the remainder of their way home. Now that they were walking and not exerting themselves as much, the frigid air was beginning to set in and the powerful gusts of wind only increased their chills.

Once the trio arrived home, Cal retreated to the guest bedroom and stretched out his fatigued muscles in solitude, eager to escape from Andrew's presence. He had forced himself to admit that his feelings for his ex were wrong last night, but having touched Andrew today like he had done so many years ago…

No, Cal scolded himself. *Don't think like that.*

After he finished stretching, Cal decided to shower off the dried sweat that had seemingly frozen to his skin. As the hot stream of water poured over his worn body, the wind continued to howl like an angry spirit against the siding of house. Cal could've sworn the floor rattled as a powerful gust surged outside, which was followed by a dull thud and scratching sounds. Several moments later, Cal heard the front door slam followed by Mr. Adams's muffled cussing. He finished washing himself and hurried out of the shower to see what the commotion was about.

"What's going on?" Cal inquired from the top of the stairs, wrapped in a towel and still dripping.

"Son of a bitch!" his father swore.

"What?" Cal repeated.

"The wind knocked a bunch of the Christmas lights off the roof," his mother called back from the kitchen while Mr. Adams continued to huff and puff.

"I spent a whole goddamn weekend putting them up."

"Todd, language," Mrs. Adams scolded her husband.

"I can fix them for you," Andrew offered.

"Andrew, your leg," Claire objected.

"It's fine now," he dismissed her concern.

"Cal, why don't you help him?" Mrs. Adams suggested.

"The roof isn't that big, Mom. I don't want to get in his way," Cal declined, and then grimaced at his pathetic excuse. "I'm sure he's got it."

"Cal," his mother repeated before she appeared at the bottom of the staircase. "Why don't you help him? It's really a two-man job."

"But Dad put them up by himself."

"Yes, which he shouldn't have done. He's not as young as he thinks he is."

"But—"

"Calvin James," his mother chided. "I don't know what has gotten into you, but you haven't been yourself the past couple of weeks. What's the deal?"

"Well, I don't want to alarm you, but the doctor recently diagnosed me with early-onset cynicism," Cal replied. Normally, he would not have copped an attitude with his mother, but her constant badgering over the past month—along with his continuous aggravation over the Andrew situation—was too much.

"Hey," she snapped.

"Yeah," he retorted and cocked an eyebrow.

"Cut the shit," she warned. "Are you trying to ruin Christmas?"

"Yes, Mom. I'm trying to ruin Christmas. I'm planning on burning the tree tonight while debating the scientific possibility of reindeer flying."

"I mean it, Scrooge, lose the attitude," his mother hissed as Cal walked away.

"Bah-fucking-humbug," he muttered under his breath.

"I heard that!" she called after him. "Watch the language, smartass."

Cal shuffled to his bedroom, with a complete lack of enthusiasm, and dried himself off before getting dressed. Despite trying to lie low and evade Andrew, everyone seemed to be pushing the two of them together, which did little to help Cal move on.

"I went to college. I work full time and pay taxes. I try to be a good person. I go to church every Sunday, for Christ's sake," he rambled aloud as he pulled on a navy turtleneck sweater. "Why are you doing this to me, God? What did I do to deserve this bad karma?"

After he dressed, Cal took a deep breath in an attempt to calm himself before going to assist Andrew with the Christmas lights. He was careful to avoid his parents as he headed downstairs and slipped outside while pulling on his coat. As he stepped out into the bitter morning, Cal was surprised to see Andrew was already working on the roof. He climbed up the ladder and joined his ex.

"You know, they say you shouldn't climb onto the roof by yourself in case something happens with the ladder," Cal stated in a flat tone when he reached the top.

"Well, I thought I was gonna be the only one up here. You know, since the roof isn't that big," Andrew retorted, but with a hint of defensiveness.

"Oh," he said, feeling slightly embarrassed that Andrew had heard the bickering between him and his mother. The two men kept their distance and refused to glance in the other's direction while Cal turned his gaze over to the jumbled mess of Christmas lights that had been twisted up in the wind.

"When I asked Claire out, I didn't know she was your sister," Andrew said after several minutes of uncomfortable silence.

"I know," Cal replied, without diverting his attention from untangling the lights.

"I mean, the last name 'Adams' is pretty common. She said she had a brother named Calvin, but—"

"I said I know. I believe you," he said with a slight edge to his voice. Andrew tossed down the strand of lights in his hand and stared at Cal.

"Then what gives?" he questioned. "Why have you been so indifferent to me?"

"Are you really asking me that?" Cal snapped. "How do you want me to act in a situation like this?"

"Well for starters, maybe you can act like you're actually giving me a chance," Andrew fired back. "Like first impressions with someone's family isn't hard enough? This is kind of awkward for me."

"Jesus Christ, here we go! Back to you as usual. Let me tell you, having you walk right back into my life has been just peachy for me. I'm *so* sorry if this is awkward for you."

"You know what I mean."

"You're right, I should act like I'm actually giving you a chance so you don't feel awkward 'cause, you know, how I feel doesn't matter," he retorted. "You know what, let's go back into the kitchen right now, and I can act like I'm giving you a chance."

"Cal—"

"Hey everyone, have you met Andrew? He's a *really* great guy. We fucked; he ghosted me, and now he's sleeping with my sister. But no hard feelings! Isn't it great that we can keep it all in the family?"

"You're so fucking immature," Andrew shouted.

"Look who's calling the kettle black."

"You're twenty-five, and you're carrying on like a child."

"Yeah well, I'm still young, but my parents have high hopes for my maturity improving since, apparently, I've mastered the sharing thing."

"Clearly you're pissed, but is this you being pissed at me as an ex or you being pissed at me as an overprotective brother?" he inquired.

"Oh, so I'm your ex now?" Cal exclaimed. "Good, glad to finally know after constantly wondering what the fuck went on between us!"

"That was over three years ago!" Andrew roared. "We were twenty and twenty-one."

The wind blew steadily as his words echoed through the air until they faded into eventual silence. Both men leered at each other, unsure of what to say next. Cal knew his ex was right; they had been young. Over the past three years, he had seen himself mature and grow up, and wasn't the same person he was at twenty-one. Though he had been scorned by Andrew, was it fair for Cal to hold a grudge? Andrew had grown up and was no longer the same person he had been three years prior. Considering this and the fact that Cal had vowed to move on from this situation the night before, he felt foolish.

"I know I acted like a little shit when we hung out," Andrew began, "but I was only twenty. I was figuring myself out, but I realize I was selfish. So I am sorry for that."

"I get it—being selfish while figuring yourself out," Cal replied in an effort to accept Andrew's apology, and he meant what he said. Though, for some reason, he couldn't form the words "it's okay."

"I know this situation isn't ideal—for either of us," he continued. "But can we try to let go of the past and move on? I mean, we don't have to be best friends or anything, but..."

"I guess we'll have to—for Claire's sake," Cal reasoned. "But it depends."

"On what?"

"Do you love her?"

"Yeah. I really do," Andrew answered without hesitation.

"Good. Then yes, we can move on," he stated.

"Thank you. I...I appreciate that. I mean it."

"You're welcome," he said before turning his attention back to the Christmas lights.

"Hey, Cal," Andrew began. "I don't know if this means anything, or if I should even say this, but if you ever want to talk about *us*—"

"*Us?*"

"Yeah, like about what happened between us—"

"No, Andrew, I don't ever want to talk about *us*," Cal dismissed him without taking his eyes off the mangled decorations. "I appreciate what you're trying to do, but I don't think it will help anything."

"Okay."

"You know what? That's a lie," he said as he set down the lights he had been working to repair. "I have a lot I want to talk about, but I'm not going to. I just want to ask you one question."

"Shoot."

"Did you—?" Cal began and chuckled under his breath, disbelieving he was about to ask this question. "Do you think if circumstances were different back then, you could've lo— You know what? Forget it."

"What were you gonna say?"

"Never mind."

"Do I think if circumstances were different back then, I could've *loved* you?" Andrew inquired. Hearing the words aloud struck a chord with Cal, and he wished he had never opened up this conversation since he was trying to make amends with Andrew.

"I don't want to know," he said curtly. "It's freezing out here. Let's hurry up and finish with these lights."

Andrew obliged and the two worked in silence on the roof. After a solid hour, Mr. Adams's Christmas lights were repaired, and Andrew and Cal retreated back into the warmth of the house, going their separate ways.

Chapter Eleven

The next couple of days were rather uneventful, and any tension in the Adams's household seemed to have dispersed. Cal and Andrew continued to honor their truce, and Cal had been making a conscious effort to appear more amicable toward his ex while in Claire's presence, per her request. The entire situation was still uncomfortable for him, but he trudged along and put his best foot forward to leave the past behind them. Despite this, Cal still made every attempt to avoid being alone with Andrew. And, of course, he had updated Sophie on the recent happenings and spoke with her frequently to stay sane.

On Tuesday evening, Cal and Claire's parents left to go to their father's company's holiday party. He had planned on spending the night alone in his room and catch up on some recreational reading. However, his plans were soon interrupted by a sudden rap on his bedroom door.

"Hey, *you*," Claire giggled as she entered with a flushed face.

"It's only nine, Claire," Cal observed. "Isn't it a little early to be drunk?"

"Oh, relax. Andrew and I are pregaming," she explained.

"Fun, fun, fun," Cal replied.

"What are you up to?"

"Just reading.

"Well, we're going to go out to the bars in a bit. You should come with us."

"Thanks for the invite, but I think I'm gonna stay in for the night."

"Yawn. You're too uptight," Claire teased. "Come out and have some fun with us."

"I'm already in sweatpants," Cal reasoned.

"Then change," his sister countered.

"Claire, really. I think I'm just going to stay in and—"

"Boo! Don't be a boring whore, Cal. Come out with us," Claire persisted. "Who knows? You might even get lucky and find yourself a fella."

"Fella? Did you actually just use the word *fella*?" Cal questioned with a laugh. "You are drunk."

"And you should be too! We're calling a car to pick us up in fifteen. See you then," she informed him before she headed back downstairs.

Cal rolled his eyes at his sister's tipsy, easygoing self. Still, he couldn't help admitting he had been growing a bit stir crazy from staying at his parents' house the past few days. While an evening out with Claire and Andrew might be awkward, it would still be a much-needed escape from his boredom.

Cal stripped out of his sweatpants and dressed himself for the bars. To Claire's delight, he met his sister and ex in the family room as they were getting ready to call for a car. After ten minutes, it arrived and the trio headed out.

Cal, Claire, and Andrew hopped between the few local bars in their semi-small town. Cal stuck to his usual draft beer while Claire and Andrew ordered various mixed drinks. Over their drinks, Claire filled Andrew in on the local geography and more noteworthy points of interest in the "downtown" area of their childhood neighborhood. By the time the group reached their fifth bar for the night, Cal had begun to feel himself edging past the point of tipsiness.

"Do you remember the time I stole your ID right after you turned twenty-one, and I tried to sneak in here?" Claire asked Cal as they settled themselves at the bar.

"What?" Andrew laughed as he took his seat between the siblings.

"Well, my hair used to be shorter back then," Claire explained with a giggle.

"But not crewcut short," Cal interjected.

"The bouncer didn't know that," she replied.

"He knew you didn't have a dick."

"Well, he didn't seem to notice because he kept staring at my tits...which is how I got in," Claire retorted and the group erupted in laughter.

"Ha ha, well you two seem to have an...*interesting* sibling relationship," Andrew commented.

"Interesting may be an understatement," Claire corrected.

"Never a dull moment with us," Cal added with a chuckle as he glanced over the draft list.

"What can I get you?" the bartender asked.

"Do you guys want to do shots?" Andrew asked.

"Ugh...I probably shouldn't," Claire began. "But it's the holidays, so why not?"

"It's on me. What do you guys want?"

"Tequila," Cal said without hesitation.

"Oh shit. We're not playing around tonight," Andrew chuckled before he handed his credit card to the bartender. "Three tequila shots, please."

"Sure thing. Do you want to leave the tab open?" he asked.

"Uh, sure."

The bartender rang the card through and then brought the shots over to the group.

"Oh, God. This is happening," Claire remarked.

"Oh, relax, Claire. Don't be a boring whore. It's the holidays," Cal teased as they picked up their shots. "Cheers."

"Cheers," Andrew replied as the two men took their shots.

"It's the holidays," Claire repeated as she braced herself for the tequila. "Holly fucking jolly."

Claire tipped her head back as she swallowed the bitter alcohol before she began coughing. She raised a hand to her mouth as her already flushed face grew redder.

"You okay?" Andrew inquired as he patted her back gently.

"No, it went down the wrong pipe," she explained between coughs. "I haven't done a tequila shot since sophomore year. I forgot how much I hate it."

Claire excused herself from the bar and hurried to the restroom.

"I better go check on her," Andrew decided. As he stood up from the bar, his hand touched Cal's hip and brushed against his lower back. As Andrew walked over to the restroom, the tequila continued to burn in Cal's chest, and he dismissed the interaction that had occurred between the two men as a simple, friendly touch.

Andrew and Claire reappeared several minutes later, and his sister was ready to call it a night. Cal—the most sober of the group—ordered a car to pick them up. By the time it arrived, Claire was nodding off, feeling the exhaustive effect of alcohol. When the trio arrived home around one in the morning, Cal and Andrew had to ease her out of the car and walk her to the front door.

"Pshh, you guys. I'm fuh-ine," Claire insisted in a slurred manner as they escorted her up the stairs.

"Be quiet, you're gonna wake Mom and Dad," Cal scolded.

"Whatever, they know we're degen—degenerates," she mumbled.

"Shh, Claire, we're almost to your room," Andrew said with a hiccup.

After a few moments, they got Claire into her bedroom and settled her into bed. She was out as soon as she hit the pillow and snored ever so slightly. Once Cal had tucked his little sister into bed, he left the room and was ready to go to sleep himself. However, as he arrived in the dimly lit hallway, he noticed Andrew had followed him.

"Is everything okay?" Cal asked, feeling tipsy and unsure as to why Andrew had followed him.

"Yeah. Yeah, everything's fine," his ex said while staring. "I, uh, I just wanted to say—"

Without warning, Andrew pressed his body against Cal's and kissed him. Caught completely off guard, Cal staggered backward and bumped into the wall with a hollow thud. Cal placed his hand on his ex's chest and shoved him away.

"Andrew, what are you doing?" he hissed as his heart pounded and legs quivered.

"You asked if I could've loved you back then," Andrew said. He once again leaned into him as he placed his hands on Cal's hips. The two men were so close now that the tips of their noses were nearly touching. "I did love you, Cal. And I still do."

"Andrew," he breathed and placed his hand on his ex's soft cheek as they pressed their foreheads together. "You're drunk."

"So are you."

"I can't. *We* can't," he reasoned as he eased himself out of Andrew's grasp. "You're with my sister."

"I know."

"It wouldn't be right," Cal reiterated as he stepped backward, away from temptation.

"I know," he repeated as he stared longingly. Cal returned his gaze as the heavy thud of his heart seemed to shake his entire body. His chest rose as he took a deep breath, hoping to gain some stability. However, all Cal breathed in was desire, and on exhaling, he released any rationality he still had.

Their bodies united, and the two men kissed each other with open mouths as Cal guided them backward through the hallway and into the guest room. Andrew closed the door behind them before ripping off his shirt. As soon as the door was shut, Cal grabbed his former lover by the belt loop of his jeans, unfastened the zipper and button, and tore them away. The ember of attraction within Cal had been reignited, and his carnal flame of lust burned ferociously.

Both men stripped before collapsing upon the bed, naked and lip-locked. Cal ran his hands over every inch of Andrew's body as a painful, yet welcoming excitement rushed through his heart. Holding his ex in his arms was just as amazing and erotic as he had remembered. Time seemed to have slipped away, and once again Cal was twenty-one, young, dumb, and in love.

He bit Andrew's lip, nibbled his earlobe, and pecked his way down from his neck to his chest. Cal circled the tip of his tongue around his nipples, tantalizing him with a craving for more. Andrew curled his toes and moaned softly—so he would not wake anyone—as he ran his hands through Cal's hair. The former lovers seemed to recall each other's favorite places to be kissed, touched, and aroused as they fooled around. The house remained still and unaware of the intimacy occurring behind closed doors.

"I missed you," Andrew said between kisses.

Cal did not respond; he couldn't. This encounter had to be physical in nature, and remain devoid of any emotional connection. If he admitted that he too had missed Andrew, then Cal would become attached once again, which he could not allow himself to do. This was to be a one-time thing, and a final goodbye between former lovers. However, being held captive in Andrew's warm embrace, Cal began to speculate that perhaps this was not a final goodbye. Despite what sensibility suggested, perhaps this could be a hello to a new beginning.

Cal traced his tongue down Andrew's torso and began kissing his waist before turning his attention toward his lover's erection. He ran his tongue around the base before he opened his jaw and took Andrew into his mouth. He replied with a pleasurable moan as Cal continued to fondle his groin with his tongue and lips.

After several minutes, Andrew's body stiffened, which—from their past experiences—Cal recognized as a sign he was getting close. However, he retreated and removed Andrew's erection from his mouth.

"You tease," Andrew toyed.

Cal chuckled as he got up from the bed, walked over to their discarded clothing, and pulled out Andrew's wallet. He fished through its contents until he found what he had been searching for—a condom—and held it up. Andrew bit his lip and cocked his eyebrows.

"I figured you'd have one," Cal said before he joined his naked lover on the bed. Once he fastened the condom on, they continued to make out for a few moments before Cal entered him.

Light beads of sweat coated the two men's bodies and they synchronized their movements as Cal thrust inside Andrew. They breathed heavy and released slight moans with each motion, careful not to disturb the late-night silence. After several minutes of lovemaking, a familiar, euphoric sensation tingled in his groin. Andrew could tell he was close to climaxing and began stroking his own erect penis. They panted with pleasure as the sensation of an orgasm grew until their bodies tensed, and they came in unison. Like before, Andrew made an odd, almost humorous face when he climaxed, rolling his eyes back and releasing his long, carnal moan, though somewhat hushed.

Cal's body grew rigid as he finished, and he remained positioned over Andrew for several moments while the two men gazed deep into each other's eyes. Finally, he and Andrew got up and cleaned themselves off, careful not to make any noise. Cal was about to pull on his boxer briefs when a pair of arms wrapped around him from behind. Andrew gave his neck a tender kiss, and chills ran up Cal's spine as he released a soft moan. He turned around to face his lover—who was also still in the buff—and stared into his brown eyes, silently wondering what was next. Andrew answered with a tender, yet passionate kiss as he eased

Cal back over to the bed. The two nestled themselves under the toasty covers as they resumed their intimacy. However, this time it was not lustful or carnal but rather, it was affectionate and gentle.

"I love you," Andrew whispered.

"I love you too," Cal replied without hesitation, despite his better judgment. For once, he wasn't thinking about the rational, proper thing to say, but instead said what he felt. He and Andrew held each other close and continued to kiss until they drifted off to sleep together.

The next morning, Cal awoke with Andrew's head resting on his furry, sculpted chest. Was this a dream? Cal could not help but recall the time, over three years ago, when the two of them had spent the night together. This time though, he had not woken up alone; he had woken up with Andrew next to him. Cal smiled with content and snuggled his lover a bit closer as he closed his eyes in an attempt to fall back to sleep.

"Cal, are you awake?" Claire inquired as she knocked on the bedroom door.

His eyes flew open as the enormity of the situation crushed Cal. He had woken up with Andrew next to him. He had woken up with his ex next to him. He had woken up with *his sister's boyfriend* next to him.

"Fuck, Andrew, wake up," Cal whispered harshly.

"Mmm, what?" Andrew groaned.

"Cal?" Claire called again.

"Shit," Andrew breathed, lurching his naked body out of bed.

"Cal, I can hear you in there," his sister said.

"Just a sec!" he called back and began to dress in a hurry. Cal lowered his voice and turned to his ex. "Fuck, we shouldn't have done this."

"We were drunk," Andrew replied as he scrambled to pull his jeans over his thick thighs.

"Yeah, but how are we gonna explain this to Claire?" he hissed. "I don't think being drunk will offset the fact that her brother and boyfriend just fucked."

"You left your phone in the hallway last night. How drunk were you?" Claire teased as the bedroom door swung open abruptly. She entered the room—both men had finished dressing themselves seconds prior to Claire's entry—and stared at Cal and Andrew. "Did you gals have a slumber party last night?"

"It was an accident," Cal began.

"Yeah, I came in here to borrow his...uh...*phone charger*," Andrew explained, "and I wound up passing out."

"Babe, your phone charger is in our room," Claire informed him.

"Yeah. Yeah it is," he replied.

"So," she began with a curious chuckle, "why didn't you use that one?"

"I thought it was going to set my phone on fire."

"What?"

"Yeah, I was pretty fucked up last night."

"Claire, you were *gone* last night. How are you up so early and not hungover?" Cal questioned, desperate to change the topic and distract his sister.

"'Cause I'm not old like you," she teased.

"Lucky bitch," he joked. "You said I left my phone in the hallway?"

"Yeah," Claire said and she held it up in her hand. "And some guy sent you a few texts. Who's Jacob?"

"What? Uh, no one," Cal replied and his face flushed in his anxiety.

"You're a bad liar. He's clearly *someone*; someone who wants to hang out tonight," his sister countered.

"Don't read my texts. Just give me my phone and get out," he said before he snatched up his cell phone.

"Hey, don't get mad at me because you got sloppy and dropped your phone in the hall. Just be glad it was me who found it and not Mom. You know how much she loves to pry," Claire said before she turned her attention to Andrew. "Babe, Mom's making breakfast."

"Okay, cool. I'll be down in a few," he replied. Claire gave the two men one last curious glance before she shrugged and left them alone.

"So..." Cal said once Claire had gone to the kitchen and was well out of earshot.

"That could've been bad," Andrew stated.

"No, this *is* bad. That could've been worse," he corrected as he shut the bedroom door gently.

"Yeah, you're right. So, um, who's Jacob?" his ex wondered aloud.

"Someone I went out with a couple of times, but it wasn't anything serious."

"Oh, good. I mean good, 'cause otherwise this might've been an even worse situation."

"Yeah. Well, I mean...like you said, we were drunk, so..."

"Yeah. We were drunk," Andrew repeated in an effort to excuse their behavior.

"Honestly, though, I wasn't that drunk."

"Me neither," Andrew admitted as he gazed at Cal with a comforting smirk.

"I'm...I'm sorry that happened," he apologized. As his dizzy mind began to sober, the gravity of the situation weighed upon him, and suffocated him with guilt and confusion.

"I'm not," Andrew revealed as he edged closer. "I know we were buzzed, but I meant what I said."

He leaned in for a kiss, but Cal retreated.

"I meant what I said too," Cal said in a lowered, shaky voice. "We can't. It's not right."

"But, you said you loved me," Andrew recalled, seeming confused as to why the two couldn't be together.

"And so does Claire. Remember? My sister—your girlfriend."

"So last night was a mistake?"

"No. Yes. I don't know," Cal sighed. "Believe me, what we did last night—I wanted it—I wanted *you*. But—it's cheating—"

"You wanted me and I wanted you. If two people want each other, shouldn't they be together?"

"Andrew, it's the same as it was back then. We both want each other, but the timing isn't right."

"What do you want?" he asked, disregarding Cal's statement.

"It doesn't matter what I want—"

"That wasn't my question. I asked what do you want?"

"I want to be with you," Cal confessed in frustration.

"And I want to be with you too."

"But we can't be together."

"Why not?" Andrew pressed.

"It's not right. You know why," Cal stated in a firm manner. He cocked his head to the side as he observed the confused expression on Andrew's face. "Do you seriously not see how this is wrong? Jesus, do you understand how a monogamous relationship works?"

"Andrew, are you coming?" Claire called from downstairs.

"Be right there," he called back before he answered Cal. "Yes, I get how it works. But I had secretly hoped maybe this could be a second chance for us."

"Andrew, you have no idea how badly I've wanted that. But these circumstances— We're gonna make Claire suspicious if we stay up here much longer," Cal reasoned. "Go downstairs and let's talk later."

Andrew agreed and left Cal alone in the guest room with his thoughts. His body and his heart craved for Andrew's affection, but not under those circumstances. It wasn't right and certainly wasn't fair for any party involved in this turbulent, everlasting affair. Cal knew he had to give his lover up. There was no way the two men could ever be together now. Even if Andrew and Claire broke up, how could he justify dating his sister's ex— especially if Cal was the reason they broke up. Feeling stressed and guilty, he retrieved his cell phone and dialed his voice of reason.

"Hey, you," Sophie greeted. "How's it going?"

"Oh, you know. It's going," he replied.

"Okay, that's not vague or anything. How are things going with fuckface?" she asked.

"Not good," Cal sighed as his grip tightened on the phone.

"Oh no, what happened?"

"I slept with him," he informed her in a hushed and hurried voice.

"Ha ha, very funny. Seriously, what's the issue?"

"Sophie," Cal said as a dizziness unrelated to his slight hangover crept upon him.

"Shut up. Cal, you did not," she dismissed him, unperturbed and still convinced he was lying to her.

He remained silent, which answered any doubts.

"*No, you didn't*," Sophie gasped.

"I slept with him, Sophie," Cal repeated gruffly.

"What—I—I don't even know what to say."

"Well, don't you want to know how it was?" he replied with humor in a desperate effort to lessen the tension.

"No, I want to know what the hell you were thinking!" she snapped. "This is Andrew we're talking about. This is your fuckboy. Even worse, this is your sister's boyfriend."

"I know," Cal acknowledged with remorse.

"When did this happen? *How* did this happen?"

"Last night. We went out to the bars—"

"*We?*"

"Andrew and I...and Claire."

"Oh, Cal—"

"We went to the bars, and when we got home, Claire passed out. And then, Andrew followed me...and it just happened."

"How drunk were you two?" Sophie questioned.

"Drunk enough to act on it...but not drunk enough to lack discretion."

"So, when you say you slept with him..."

"We had sex."

"Oh shit," Sophie mumbled. "Honestly, Cal. I love you, but I'm at a complete loss of words here. I mean, I don't know what to say about this."

"Me neither," he admitted.

"Did you guys talk this morning?" she inquired. "Assuming that, you know, he didn't leave once you fell asleep like last time."

"Ha ha, very funny," Cal replied. "Yes, he stayed in bed with me overnight. And we talked a bit this morning."

"Well?"

"He sounded like he wants to be with me."

"Cal, no."

"I know, I told him it was wrong and we can't be together..." Cal started and his voice waivered. His eyes stung as fresh tears formed and he pinched the corners of his eyes, desperate to keep the tears from falling. "But, Sophie, I really want to be with him."

"You can't let this happen again. You can't repeat what happened years ago," she said firmly. "It doesn't matter what he says; he's a manipulator."

"He told me he loved me," he countered and felt foolish saying it aloud. Still, he hung onto this notion, hoping it could be true.

"Cal, I love you. Your family loves you. Claire loves you. Jacob may even love you if you give him the chance to. But Andrew—"

"He doesn't love me?" Cal retorted.

"Listen to me, Cal, he is a fuckboy. We both know it. Look at what he put you through."

"Things were complicated back then. The timing wasn't right," he reasoned defiantly.

"And the timing is right now?" Sophie shot back. "When you love someone, you fight for them—no matter how complicated. In my eyes, Andrew never fought for you when he could've. And that's his loss.

"But now, here's Jacob. And it seems to me he's fighting for you. He's been patient with you and receptive to your situation. Now, I'm not saying you guys are going to be together forever, but he's someone who doesn't want to play games. You can't let yourself fall for people who want to play games. You can't let yourself fall for Andrew."

"I know," Cal muttered.

"I know you know, but you're still falling for him," she replied in a somewhat harsh tone and an uncomfortable silence fell upon the two friends. "I'm gonna be tied up at a Christmas party with some of my college friends today. But how about I come over tonight? Does your mom's invitation still stand?"

"Yeah, of course. You're always welcome here. I'm pretty sure she likes you more than she likes Claire and I."

"Well I am pretty great, aren't I?" she joked. "But anyway, I'll come over later and stay till Christmas to help you get through this."

"Thanks, Sophie."

"You're welcome. Now, keep your dick in your pants till I get there," Sophie teased.

"Oh, kinky. I love it when you sweet-talk me," Cal replied.

"Shut up, you know what I mean," she laughed. "No more kissing Andrew. Got it?"

"Got it."

After Cal hung up, he figured it would be best to lay low that day until he and Andrew had a chance to talk in private. His parents had been popping in and out of the house all day, running errands and finishing their last-minute Christmas shopping. Mrs. Adams tended to get a little frazzled when preparing for company, and having the extended family over for Christmas in two days had her in a state of upheaval. Claire—not as immune to hangovers as she previously thought—had begun to feel the unforgiving effects of last night's binge. By early afternoon, she had taken refuge in the silence of her bedroom to nurse a relentless headache.

With his sister detained and his parents' sporadic appearances, Cal seized advantage of the moment to coordinate a time and place to discuss with Andrew what had happened and how to handle it. Sophie had texted Cal to say she wouldn't make it to his family's house until around ten, so the two men decided to grab a drink early that evening at Crush, a local gay bar in the town over.

Just after seven, he and Andrew broke away from the house, and Cal drove them to the bar. Despite the parking lot being somewhat vacant since it was still early, Crush's radiant signs welcomed and invited the two inside. The bar was quaint and dimly lit, decorated by exotic-looking plants and provocative, neon pictures. Cal and Andrew settled themselves at the bar, which was opposite from the dance floor at the other end of the building where a live band was setting up and testing their instruments instead of the usual DJ stand.

"Seems like an interesting place," Andrew remarked.

"It is. It's the only gay bar in the area, so it brings in an interesting crowd...but it's great," Cal responded.

"Oh yeah?"

"Yeah, it's the first gay bar I went to—my eighteenth birthday."

"Ha, I feel like that's a rite of passage for every gay boy," Andrew teased.

"Ha ha, I guess so. What are you drinking?"

"I'm good with whatever."

Cal ordered them draft beers, and once their drinks arrived, the two somberly discussed their *predicament*. Though Cal was torn inside, he attempted to remain strong. The former lovers reflected on their past fling from years earlier, chatted about Andrew's relationship with Claire, and evaluated where the two of them currently stood. Though neither could deny their attraction to the other, Cal forced Andrew to acknowledge that what they had was not right.

"Are we okay?" Andrew asked his ex.

"Yeah, we're good," Cal reassured him as he took a swig of beer. "As long as we don't sleep with each other again."

"So I guess we should stay away from each other when we're drunk," he laughed.

"If that's the case, we better avoid each other during the big boozing holidays."

"So, New Year's, St. Paddy's Day..."

"Mardis Gras. You know, the essentials," Cal chuckled.

"All right. Glad we've got that settled," Andrew said. "You know, it's good we can laugh about this but...I'm not sorry last night happened. I know it's not right—and don't get me wrong—I love your sister—but I really do love you."

"Well, apparently there's something about us Adams kids. People can't seem to get enough of us," Cal replied before tossing back the remainder of his beverage.

"Cal, I'm being serious. I know it's not right, and we're moving on from this, but I want you to know that," Andrew insisted as he stared into his ex's eyes.

"Thanks, Andrew. I appreciate that—and I'm not being a smart ass. I mean it, I love you too," he said as he returned his longing stare.

"Hi there, handsome." A man appearing to be in his early thirties, with bleached blond hair, trendy clothes, and an obnoxious blinged-out gold chain stumbled over to Cal and Andrew. "I'm Austin. You boys seem familiar; come here often?"

"No," Cal replied curtly, unable to hide his impatience. Though he did not know Austin personally, Cal did recognize him from social media—they had several gay, mutual friends online—and he had no desire to chat. Austin was giving off a vibe that indicated his personality was as fake as his showy persona.

Cal had met this type of guy before and assumed he had Austin figured out: he was the type of guy to utilize dating apps for the sole purpose of gaining followers and likes on social media in an effort to be *known* in the gay community. Guys like Austin tended to be into the *scene*: frequently going to clubs, hooking up, and dabbling with drugs. Cal could respect the whole "to each their own" mantra, but personally, he had no patience dealing with these types of guys—especially at a critical moment like this.

"You seem familiar," Austin repeated as he stirred his blue cocktail with a straw. "Oh, I know where I've seen you before! You're on *Sleazr*."

"Not since college." Cal dismissed him with a dry laugh.

"What about you?" he asked Andrew before taking a large gulp of his drink.

"Uh—"

"Neither of us live around here, so I think you've got us confused with someone else," Cal interjected. "Now I'm sorry, but we're kind of in the middle of something here."

Austin stared at Cal for a moment until he was distracted by the appearance of an acquaintance entering the bar. Quickly forgetting why he had approached Cal and Andrew, he hurried off to greet his friend, and the two then disappeared within the now-growing crowd.

"Well, that was...random," Andrew said.

"Nice to know we've still got it though," Cal laughed.

"Ha ha yeah. So anyway...last night was goodbye?"

"I guess so."

"Oh, okay."

"Honestly, I don't know what it was," Cal admitted.

"Me neither," Andrew concurred. "Maybe we should actually say goodbye? So we both know we're actually saying goodbye."

"I'm not saying goodbye like that again."

"Well, how about we say goodbye like *this*."

Andrew leaned forward on his bar stool and kissed Cal on the lips. He responded by opening his mouth, and the two shared a final, tender kiss that lasted for several moments. Cal broke away and forced himself to plunge back into reality.

"Goodbye, Cal," his ex said.

"Goodbye, Andrew" he replied with a weak, bittersweet smile. "So, another round?"

"Yeah, but this time it's on me."

"Hey, Cal?" a voice called. He turned on his stool and saw Jacob waving to him from the entrance.

"Oh shit," Cal muttered.

"Do you know him?" Andrew asked to the side as Jacob approached them at the bar.

"Jacob!" Cal greeted a little too enthusiastically and gave him a hug.

"Hey, what are you doing here?" Jacob inquired.

"Wouldn't you know it? This is the nearest gay bar to my parents' house. I used to come here when I was in high school," Cal clarified in a nonchalant tone. "What about you?"

"I'm here for my friend's gig tonight," he explained.

"I'm sorry, what?"

"My friend's gig...the one I texted you about."

"Oh, *that* gig," Cal recalled as his stomach lurched. "The band."

"Yeah, my friend's."

"Right, your friend's band! Your friend's band is playing *here*...tonight. Ha ha, what are the odds? Small world we live in, huh?" he rambled.

"You know, I never did hear back from you," Jacob commented with a sheepish grin.

"Yeah, I'm sorry. Things got kind of crazy at home," Cal justified.

"It's cool. I figured you were busy," he replied. "How is everything going with *that* situation?"

"Oh, you know. I'm trying my best to deal with it."

"Well, luckily the holidays will be over soon," Jacob reassured him before eyeing Andrew. "I'm sorry, we're completely ignoring—"

"Oh, this is my friend," Cal introduced.

"Hi, I'm Jacob," he greeted as he shook Andrew's hand.

"Hey, I'm Andrew."

"Oh, uh, *Andrew*. Nice to meet you. Well, I better go find my friends," Jacob stammered before he turned and left in haste. Cal's discomfort shifted to guilt as Jacob walked away seeming dejected.

"Here's your beer," Andrew stated as the bartender delivered their drinks.

"I'm good for right now. Um, I'll be right back," Cal said as he eased his way into the crowd that was gathering by the band. "Jacob, wait."

"Forget it, Cal," he retorted as he continued his way up to the stage.

"It's not what you think!"

Jacob stopped abruptly and spun around to face Cal.

"I saw you two kiss!"

"Oh," Cal said.

"You know what? If you were seeing other guys, then fine. We haven't been seeing each other that long, and we haven't talked about being exclusive. But *him*? Honestly, Cal!"

"I'm sorry."

"Don't feel sorry for me," Jacob exclaimed. "Feel sorry for your sister. And, more importantly, feel sorry for yourself—that you don't respect yourself enough to admit you deserve better than him."

"What?" Cal scoffed as he was both taken aback by the shift in Jacob's usual easygoing demeanor and offended by the insult.

"Don't pretend you don't know it's true," Jacob stated. "You know, when we first met, you seemed like a genuine guy. But then you'd get quiet on me off and on, and you assured me we were good. And now, *this*? Cal, from what you've told me, you're acting just like Andrew."

"That's not fair," Cal muttered, at a loss for words. A sudden sadness resulting from Jacob's accusation settled over him, and he was deeply hurt, but more so concerned. Was Jacob right? Was he being selfish and acting like Andrew?

"No? You know what else isn't fair? Walking in and seeing someone you cared about making out with their fuckboy ex, who they're clearly still not over," Jacob spat. "Bye, Cal."

"Wait, it's not like that!" he shouted, but it was too late and Jacob stormed off, leaving Cal alone. The guilt he was feeling was immense.

"Everything okay?" Andrew asked as he approached Cal through the crowd.

"Yeah, just fine," he lied. "You know, I'm actually not feeling the greatest. Do you want to leave soon?"

"Uh yeah, sure."

"I'm sorry, I know it's early but..."

"Don't worry. I've got to run an errand anyway."

Cal and Andrew finished their beers, closed out the tab at the bar, and exited Crush in a hurry. Andrew offered to drive home, which Cal appreciated, because he was a bit shaky from his encounter with Jacob since he was not a very confrontational person. On the drive home, he texted Sophie to fill her in on that night's drama and informed her he'd be home in half an hour.

Once the two men arrived at the house, Andrew handed over the keys to Cal, and they retreated to their separate rooms. Claire was asleep on the couch in front of the television, and his parents were nowhere to be found—probably out running last-minute errands of their own or at a neighbor's house for a holiday celebration. Cal appreciated the silence and tranquility that gave him time to sulk alone in his bedroom and reflect on his misdoings.

He sank into his bed and buried his face in the pillow before he sighed in despair. How could he have done this to Jacob? Cal realized now that he had only thought about himself when it came to Andrew and had failed to factor in Jacob's and Claire's own feelings. He had created a mess and—worst of all—he had ruined things between him and Jacob.

His sulking was interrupted by a familiar *ping*. Cal reached for his phone, but he had no messages or notifications. The *ping* sounded again before a door closed at the end of the hallway. Cal realized it was not his own phone *pinging*, though that noise sounded so familiar. Where had he heard it before?

"*Sleazr*," he said aloud in apparent realization.

Cal's phone began to vibrate on the nightstand as Sophie's name appeared on its screen. He scrambled to retrieve it and answered on the third ring.

"Yeah?"

"I'm here," Sophie informed him.

"Okay, good. Come upstairs—*quick*."

"What?"

"Just do it," he hissed before hanging up. A few moments later, the front door squeaked open followed by light footsteps ascending the staircase. "I'm in here."

"Cal?" Sophie said as she peeked into his guest bedroom.

"Shh," he scolded as he yanked her in and shut the door behind them.

"Cal, what is going on?" she wondered.

"Andrew is on *Sleazr*," he revealed.

"How do you know?" Sophie inquired.

"I heard his phone go off before; it was a notification from *Sleazr*."

"Are you sure?"

"Positive; I know what I heard," Cal assured. "Give me your phone. I'll prove it."

"Why not use yours?" she questioned as she fished her phone out of her purse.

"Because, if I open the app on my phone it'll activate my old profile, and he'll know it's me," Cal reasoned as he took Sophie's phone from her. He downloaded the *Sleazr* app with haste and created a quick, pictureless profile. Then, he browsed through nearby guys and, sure enough, Andrew's face appeared.

"Oh my God," Sophie gasped.

"That fucker!" Cal exclaimed.

"What does his profile say?" she pressed.

"Brown eyes; five-foot-nine," Cal read aloud from the profile. "A hundred and fifty pounds? Bullshit! Maybe three years ago before he got that dad bod."

"Anything else?"

"His *About Me* says, 'Not sure what I'm looking for. Hit me up if you're chill.'"

"Do you think he's actually using *Sleazr*? Like, meeting up with guys from the app?" Sophie asked in disbelief.

"I'm not sure, but let's find out." Cal opened the internet browser on Sophie's phone and searched for pictures of cute, young men. He found a photo that appeared realistic and not posed, and saved it to the phone. Then, he reopened *Sleazr* and cropped the saved photo to fit as his profile picture. Once he had saved his changes, he messaged Andrew.

"Hey sexy, how are you?" Sophie read aloud from the phone. "Does that shit actually work on there?"

"Sometimes," Cal admitted. Sophie's phone—which was silenced—vibrated to announce their fake *Sleazr* profile had received a message.

"What does it say?"

"Ew," Cal grimaced. "It's not from him; it's some old guy. All he said was 'tasty.'"

"Ew, really?"

"Yeah. Sorry, pal, I'm not into cannibalism," Cal remarked. "Oh wait, here we go. Andrew said he's good."

"Well, that doesn't give us a lot to go off of," Sophie determined.

"Fortunately, this app isn't usually about conversations," Cal clarified as he messaged back.

"What are you saying?"

"I'm asking what he's looking for."

"'Nothing serious. Just looking and seeing what comes my way.' What does that mean?" Sophie questioned with an edge to her voice.

"It means he's fucking us both over: me and Claire," Cal muttered in disbelief.

He had so desperately wanted to believe that Andrew had matured and that he had actually loved Cal—years ago and now. However, he came to the forced realization he had been played...again. The inner conflict he had faced when he left college for his first job, the sleepless nights spent pondering whether or not he had made the right decision to leave, the loneliness and isolation, the numerous dates that had left Cal missing Andrew, the three and a half years of emotional distress had all been caused by a fuckboy; someone who had never given and would never give two shits about him.

Though Cal always suspected Andrew had played him, he was never able to confirm it. And with recent events, he actually believed Andrew had loved him and still loved him. However, it had all been a lie—their entire "relationship"—and Cal felt a familiar sense of grief—the same as he had experienced when Andrew first broke his heart. This time though, the grief was accompanied by a rage that had been buried for years.

"Oh my God," Cal spat in apparent understanding. "When we were out earlier, he said he had to run an errand tonight."

"Do you think he's meeting up with someone tonight?" Sophie gasped. "What are you going to do? Should you tell Claire?"

"I'll tell you what I'm gonna do; I'm gonna beat the shit out of that motherfucker," he snarled as he cast Sophie's phone aside and reached for the door.

"Cal, no!" Sophie cried as she hurried after her friend. She caught him before he was able to throw the door open and yanked on his arm. "Stop!"

"Get off!"

"This isn't going to help anything."

"Only one way to find out."

"Cal," Sophie hissed so they would not alert Andrew to their presence. She pulled on Cal's arm, which was still grasping the doorknob, and spun him around to face her, causing the door to open slowly. "Breathe and think. What's going to happen if you go and confront Andrew right now? You're going to punch him and then what? How are you going to explain that to Claire and your parents?"

"So what? I'm supposed to let him get away with this?"

"No, but *this* is not the way to handle it."

"So what do you suggest we do then?"

"I'm not sure, but—"

The bedroom door creaked open and Andrew stepped out into the hallway. He must not have heard their discussion, since he seemed surprised to see them both standing in the open doorway of the guest bedroom as he walked by.

"Hey there," Andrew greeted as he pocketed his cell phone and car keys. "What's up?"

"Oh, we were just trying to figure out a movie to watch tonight," Sophie lied.

"Oh cool," he replied. "Um, I don't think we've met."

"This is Andrew," Cal introduced.

"Oh, Andrew. I've heard a lot about you," she said with a subtle tone of disgust.

"Uh, you have?"

"Yeah...from Claire. I'm a family friend."

"Oh, okay," Andrew said before a momentary, awkward silence fell upon the trio. "I'm sorry, I still don't know your name."

"Sophie. I'm Sophie," she stated with a stiff handshake.

"Nice to meet you—"

"So, where are you going?" Cal asked impatiently.

"What?"

"You said earlier that you were going to run an errand tonight."

"Oh...oh yeah!" Andrew replied. "Yeah, I'm running out to the store to grab a last minute Christmas present."

"At this hour?" Cal questioned with a faked pleasantry.

"Yeah, a lot of stores have extended holiday hours."

"Really? Even this late? It might be closed by the time you get there."

"I'll risk it," Andrew said.

"Well, you're a brave man," Cal responded.

"It's not a big deal," he shrugged before he shot Cal a curious expression. Andrew pulled on his coat and then brushed past Cal and Sophie.

"I guess it's not for you," Cal muttered under his breath.

"I think Claire is still asleep. Let her know I'm out running an errand if she wakes up and asks," Andrew stated.

"Oh, I will," he called after his ex.

"Ew, that's the guy you've been crying over?" Sophie asked Cal once Andrew was well out of earshot since she had only seen pictures of him on social media.

"Sophie, not now," Cal retorted.

"All I'm saying is you can do a lot better. He's not even that attractive."

"Sophie—"

"He does have a cute ass though; I'll give you that."

"Okay, that's a conversation for another day. Let's deal with the issue at hand: this prick is cheating on my sister."

"You're right; I'm sorry. So, how do we prove he's meeting up with someone?" Sophie wondered.

Chapter Twelve

Three years earlier

November transitioned into a brisk December, and with two weeks left until graduation, Cal was in the process of packing up his apartment. When he was not packing, he was in the company of his friends so they could all enjoy Cal's remaining time with them, which also helped to keep his mind off Andrew.

One day, while he was in the midst of packing up his extensive CD collection, Andrew texted him:

> *Hey just wanted to say good luck on your last set of finals ever!!*

What's he playing at? Cal wondered.

The two hadn't spoken since their last date, which was nearly a month ago. Had Andrew decided he wanted him again? Even if he had, it was too late since Cal was all set to graduate soon, and he would be moving to his new apartment the day after that.

> *Thanks you too!!*

Andrew continued to text him that day, but Cal kept his responses brief and steered clear of the conversation venturing anywhere toward the topic of them hanging out again. For the sake of his mental well-being, he could not allow himself to play any more of Andrew's games.

The following week, Cal's parents and sister, along with several members of his extended family and a couple of close family friends, made the trek out to his college town in advance of Cal's impending graduation. The night before the ceremony, Cal and his company celebrated early with light refreshments in the lounge of the hotel they were staying at. They were to have a larger graduation party with Cal's college friends the next day, following the ceremony.

Cal left the hotel and arrived at his barren apartment just after seven that evening. He put on the tea kettle and then removed his business-casual attire, which he replaced with fleece sweatpants and a loose-fitting graphic tee. He gazed around at the various cardboard boxes scattered around his mostly packed-up apartment. He took in the sight of its emptiness and the realization of the coming graduation sank in.

The high-pitched whistle of the boiling kettle drew Cal back to the kitchen, and he poured himself a cup of green tea. He allowed the bitter tea leaves to steep in the steaming liquid for several minutes before he tossed the tea bag in the trash. Then, Cal grasped the warm mug, exited the kitchen, and settled himself in front of a window. He stared out into the night that had settled over his college town and watched the twinkling headlights of cars passing by. As he shifted his gaze from the roads to the towering buildings, Cal felt a pang of regret. Never in his wildest dreams had he ever considered making this place his home, but now that he was about to leave, he wished he could stay.

A sudden knock at the apartment door drew Cal's attention. He set his cup of tea on a nearby box and made his way over to the door. Intrigued, he opened it to find Andrew standing in front of him.

"Wh—what? How did you get over here?" was all Cal was able to stammer.

"I took a bus," Andrew stated and smiled weakly. "Can I come in?"

"Why?" he responded, willing himself not to break now that he was in love's presence.

"I get that you're probably pissed at me...and I don't blame you. I've been acting like a little bitch lately," Andrew admitted. "Can I please come in?"

Cal remained silent and eyed him with suspicion.

"I'm sorry I've been quiet. I've been trying to protect myself over the past few months because I've been falling for you," Andrew confessed. "But no matter how hard I try, I can't stay away."

"I'm moving in two days. I really want to let you in," he began in a shaky voice, "but I can't do that until I know what's going on between us."

"Can't we talk about that tomorrow?"

"No, we can't! I've had enough of your games!" Cal exclaimed, his voice reverberating through the empty hall. Both he and Andrew were caught off guard by his unexpected outburst, and the latter stared at the floor. "I'm not letting you in until I know what's going on between us. You owe me that."

"You're right," Andrew mumbled before he fell silent for a moment.

"Well?" Cal pressed.

"I think that's going to be a serious conversation to have, and I really want to be with you. Can we just enjoy tonight and then talk about this in the morning?"

Cal remained unconvinced of his intentions until Andrew finally gazed up at him with those seductive brown eyes.

"I *really* want to be with you," Andrew repeated. "I want you."

Before Cal realized it, the door was slammed shut and the two men held each other in a passionate embrace within the apartment. They staggered over stray objects and stumbled into moving boxes as Cal guided him to the bed, stripping each other of their clothing along the way.

He laid him on the bed and kissed him as his tongue explored Andrew's mouth once again. Cal's toned arms wrapped around the young man's body, unwilling to ever let him go again. The last four months had been filled with angst as Cal attempted to make sense of what was going to happen next. What would happen after he graduated? What would happen if he relocated for a job? What would happen between him and Andrew?

Despite the more pressing matters that had been dealt with that final semester of college, Andrew was still at the front of Cal's mind constantly. He was always waiting for Andrew, wondering when he might receive a text or ever have the opportunity to see him again. Now that he was here in his apartment, making out on the bed surrounded by various boxes packed with personal belongings and memories, Cal's mind wanted to make sense of what was going to happen next. Was Andrew only going to be here for a moment or for the night? And what was going to happen after this rekindling?

Perhaps Cal had been naïve over the past four months and had made too much of the time he had shared with Andrew. He recognized that they were both young, and the handful of "dates" they had did not constitute serious dating. This certainly wasn't a relationship, and maybe it wasn't anything more than a simple fling despite how strongly he felt about Andrew.

Cal willed his mind to be silent as he rediscovered Andrew's body. In that moment, what was and what could be didn't matter anymore. All Cal cared about was that the first man he had ever truly fallen for—the first man he had ever shared this much of his body with—was in his arms again. Cal broke away for a moment and stared longingly into his brown eyes as he ran the back of his hand over Andrew's smooth cheek, remembering the warmth of his touch.

They resumed their intimacy, kissing, teasing, and fondling each other as their bodies reconnected. Cal and Andrew both grew hard and soon yearned for more. They communicated through deep moans, and Andrew placed his legs on Cal's shoulders, like he had done almost two months prior. Only this time, it wasn't just a demonstration. This time, both men were completely nude, and their hearts longed for each other.

Although Cal had never done anything like this before, he moved to retrieve lubrication and protection from a box he had purposely kept hidden under his bed. His head raced with thoughts, but he was quick to silence them as he focused on the sight of his naked lover in front of him. Finally, Cal entered him and Andrew groaned in pleasure.

Beads of sweat began to coat Cal's flushed face as he rocked his pelvis back and forth rhythmically. Andrew grasped the wooden rods of the headboard behind him as he gyrated in sync with each thrust. Cal panted as he made love to Andrew, their skin growing damp with perspiration from their passion.

The two moaned with each motion, kiss, and heartbeat. Soon, a euphoric sensation began to tingle in Cal's groin. Andrew must have been close to climaxing because he began to fondle his own erection. Cal's heart thudded as the sensation of an impending orgasm gripped him. He could not hold it back any longer and allowed himself to let go with a grunt of ecstasy. His body tensed as warm spurts of semen were released into the condom, and Andrew arched his back, moaning as Cal came inside him. Andrew continued stroking his own penis until he too climaxed, nearly concurrent with Cal. As he came, Cal noticed that Andrew made an odd—and almost humorous—face while his eyes rolled back, and he released a long, carnal sigh.

Cal collapsed onto his back next to Andrew. Feeling satisfied, they struggled to catch their breath as the gratifying sensation they experienced lingered. Andrew turned to face Cal with an alluring smile, and the two lovers shared a tender kiss. Then, he lay his head on Cal's chest, and they soon drifted off into sleep.

The next morning, Cal awoke naked and alone in his bed. He gazed around his empty apartment to discover that Andrew was nowhere to be seen, and his discarded clothes were gone. He had left. There had been no conversation; no goodbye. Just as he had done numerous times before, Andrew popped in and out of Cal's life when it was convenient for him. He had left, and this time there would never be a future reunion; Andrew was gone.

The rest of that day was a confusing blur to Cal. He barely recalled crossing the stage to receive his diploma at graduation. His heart, weary from four months of Andrew's toying with him, ached like never before. He had given his all, both physically and emotionally, to Andrew and had received nothing in return, not even a goodbye.

Despite the routine heartbreaks, Cal had told no one except Sophie about Andrew. His lover, who had hurt him repeatedly, was now merely a fragment in Cal's mind that would haunt him. However, Cal continued to force a foolish smile as his family and friends congratulated him, unaware of the previous night's events—unaware of his four-month-long affair.

The next day, Cal and his family loaded up a moving truck with all of the possessions that he had packed over the past two weeks. Within a few hours, his place was utterly bare as if he had never even lived there. Confused, broken, and feeling as empty as his apartment, Cal handed over his key in the building's leasing office. Then, he got into his car and drove off into the grim future, allowing himself only one quick glance back at the college town where he so desperately craved to stay.

Chapter Thirteen

Cal and Sophie hurried downstairs—past Claire, who was still napping on the couch as she recovered from her hangover—and slipped out the side door as Andrew started up his car. They watched the glow of headlights back out of the driveway and then ride off into the night. Cal and Sophie sprang toward the latter's car—so as not to be easily identified—and sped after Andrew. They maintained a natural distance to avoid suspicion and followed him down the main street.

Andrew merged onto the nearby highway and drove west for about ten minutes until he took the exit into a neighboring town. Cal and Sophie tailed him through a tranquil suburb—which glowed with holiday lights and décor—as they wondered about Andrew's destination. Finally, he turned into a driveway that led to a community of townhouses.

"Don't turn here," Cal instructed. "Drive past the entrance."

"Are you sure?" Sophie asked.

"Yeah, I don't want him to see us. We can loop around and then pull in there. We'll look for his car."

Sophie followed Cal's instructions and drove them through the neighborhood once more. When they approached the townhouses, Sophie turned on her blinker and pulled into the community. She steered through the development as they scanned for Andrew's car and, after a short search, they found it parked outside a townhouse toward the end of the road. Sophie parked a few cars ahead of it and then killed her engine.

"Can I see your phone?" Cal inquired.

"Yeah," she replied and she retrieved it from her purse. Cal took the phone and opened *Sleazr* before browsing through nearby men.

"Here's Andrew's profile. It says he's 297 feet away," Cal informed her.

"Ew, Mr. Right Now?" Sophie squealed as she read the profile name of the mystery man in the townhouse.

"Yeah, great profile name," he scoffed. "So Andrew is in there somewhere with Mr. Right Now."

"What do we do?"

"We wait for him to come out."

"And then?"

"I'm not sure," Cal admitted.

He and Sophie both fell silent as they eyed the row of homes from the car and waited. Despite his solemn demeanor, a vengeful anger boiled within Cal as he criticized himself for being played by Andrew not once, but twice. Images of his ex and a sleazy, aroused stranger fornicating in the townhouse relentlessly played through Cal's mind, only increasing his anger—which quelled any heartache he may have experienced. While he did not know how to handle this situation, Cal knew he would not allow himself to be a victim any longer.

Two silhouettes appeared within an upper level window of the townhouse; it appeared as though they were dressing. Sophie and Cal observed from the car as a window lit up on the ground floor, followed by the porch light. The front door opened as Andrew and a man—who appeared to be in his early thirties, with pasty skin and a buzz cut—stepped outside for a final embrace. Without thinking, Cal stormed out of the car as he witnessed the two men kissing and approached them with Sophie at his heels. Cal did not have the faintest clue what he would do or say, but prowled over as adrenaline pulsed through his veins.

"Oh hey, Andrew," he shouted in a fake cheery voice. "What are the odds of bumping into you here?"

"Cal?" Andrew sputtered.

"Who the fuck are you?" the stranger questioned.

"Hey, Mr. Right Now. I'm Cal," he greeted. His heart thumped in anticipation of confronting Andrew, a mix of anger and dread causing the discomfort. Nevertheless, Cal continued his showdown, refusing to allow anyone to walk over him or Claire. "Did you use up all your libido on this fuckboy? Or are you up for another round?"

"Did you follow me here?" Andrew asked in disbelief.

"Yep," Cal said with a smile. "Did this guy get a taste of me? You know, since we fucked last night."

"Oh shit. Are you his boyfriend?" the man inquired, unease evident in his voice.

"No, I'm his ex," he replied in a matter-of-fact tone. "He's dating my sister now."

"What!" he exclaimed in shock as his once-pasty face flushed. "But, you said you were single—"

"Oh, did he?"

"Shut up, Craig," Andrew hissed.

"Don't say that. I want to hear what *Craig* has to say," Cal stated with a malicious smile. "Go ahead, Craig."

"I swear he said he was single, and he was just looking for fun; no strings attached," the man chattered in a flustered manner, clearly unprepared for the situation he had been drawn into. "I'm so sorry."

"Don't be. You didn't know. Besides, this is what Andrew does."

"What the fuck is that supposed to mean?" Andrew spat as he stepped off the porch. Cal's legs shook, and his stomach churned as his ex approached, staring him in the eye with resentment. While he may have felt inferior to Andrew in the past, he refused to bow down in silence and watch his former lover escape the consequences of his crimes.

"It means you do what you want to and don't care about who you string along and who you hurt," Cal retorted in a raised voice that was surprisingly strong despite his gentle nature, trembling body, and worn-out heart. It was as though Andrew's emotional weight had evaporated, cleansing the depression, guilt, and heartache that had accumulated since his ex first sleazed his way into Cal's stable life.

"Oh my God, are you still talking about what happened when we were in undergrad?"

"I'm talking about what's happening right now!" he countered. "What I care about is that things haven't changed. It's been three and a half fucking years, and you haven't changed except now you're fucking over my sister."

"You don't understand—"

"No, I don't!" Cal interjected. "I don't understand and honestly, I don't care anymore. You're not worth wasting the energy of trying to figure you out. You've played your games with me already, but don't you dare go sleeping around while you're with my sister."

Andrew took a deep breath as he glared at Cal.

"And while you're at it, get tested you washed-up slut," he chided.

"Fuck you, Cal!" Andrew swore before he marched away toward his car.

"I'm gonna tell her," he threatened.

Andrew whipped around.

"What?"

"I'm gonna tell her," Cal repeated.

"Please, don't."

"Why shouldn't I? How is this fair to her?"

"It's not," Andrew admitted.

"Exactly, so I'm telling Claire."

"No. Let me tell her...please," Andrew requested.

"How do I know you're actually going to? I mean, you don't have the best track record with telling the truth."

"I will. Believe me."

"When?" Cal demanded.

"I don't know."

"Well, I need to know, or else I'm telling Claire tonight."

"Okay, okay. Tomorrow is Christmas Eve, and then all of your family is coming Christmas Day. Give me until the day after to tell her," Andrew reasoned.

"Fine. But I mean it; if you don't tell her, I will," Cal warned. Andrew nodded his head in understanding before the two men walked away in opposite directions, leaving Sophie and Craig in stunned silence. The two stood awkwardly on the porch for a moment longer as they avoided making eye contact.

"Um, happy holidays," Sophie said to Craig with a slight wave before she hurried after Cal to the car. Craig remained on the porch in the frigid evening air, as he continued to process the altercation that had just occurred.

*

As a result of recent events, the usual cheer and joy associated with the Christmas holiday was absent that year for Cal. Instead, anger and resentment clutched his spirit as he willed the holidays to end. Come December twenty-sixth, Cal would be in the comfort of his own apartment, and he hoped Andrew would be out of the Adamses' lives for good.

Meanwhile, Sophie had opted to stay at the family's home for Christmas Eve and Day—per the family matriarch's insistence—since her own parents were already on their cruise. The two friends kept to themselves, as they made sure to avoid Andrew after their confrontation. Pleasantries at the family's traditional Feast of the Seven Fishes dinner were exaggerated between the three, to avert suspicion from the rest of the Adams clan—who still remained unaware of the history between Cal and Andrew.

The Christmas Day celebrations with the immediate family were limited since Mrs. Adams had various preparations to complete before their relatives were scheduled to arrive early that afternoon. Therefore, the family exchanged gifts before Mrs. Adams returned to tidying up the dining room and setting the table with ornate china. She assigned several tasks to Cal and Sophie as well, while Claire and Andrew retreated to their bedroom. Finally, the doorbell rang just after two o'clock, signaling their guests' arrival.

"Here we go," Cal muttered to Sophie before he opened the front door to greet the family. His maternal grandmother entered first with his younger cousin, Troy, followed by his mother's sister and brother and their spouses. Within moments, the house was abuzz with chatter and cheer as the relatives embraced one another.

"Hi, Grandma Pearl," Cal greeted as he received a tight hug from her.

"Oh, Cal, you look great. And, Miss Sophie, it's so good to see you," Pearl remarked. "Are you two finally together?"

"Um," Sophie began.

"No," Cal interjected. "I've told you before, Sophie has a boyfriend."

"Are you two engaged?" his grandmother pried.

"Um, no. Not yet," Sophie replied with a muffled bitterness, while Claire and Andrew made their way downstairs to welcome the family.

"Well, nothing is final until there's a ring on your finger," Pearl continued before she lowered her voice and winked. "And even then, it comes right off."

Sophie bit her lip to conceal a giggle as she blushed.

"Okay, Grandma, have you met Claire's boyfriend?" Cal inquired as he steered his grandmother toward Claire's direction, hoping that the announcement of a significant other would captivate Pearl's attention to veer her off the current discussion.

"Why did your grandmother ask if we were together?" Sophie whispered to Cal once Pearl was out of earshot.

"She doesn't know," he said.

"You never told her?" she asked.

"No. It turns out she's kind of conservative, so it's better that she doesn't know. Besides, she's not going to live forever."

"Cal, that's terrible!"

"What? Don't get me wrong, I love her...but it's the truth. It's easier this way," he reasoned. "I've actually never talked with the extended family about it, so I don't know if anyone other than my parents and Claire knows. But at this rate, I'm going to die alone anyway, so it doesn't matter."

"Oh, Claire, *this* is your boyfriend?" his grandmother's voice sounded above the chatter. "Is he a Mexican? He looks Mexican."

"Um, the politically correct term is Hispanic," Cal's Aunt Evelyn chimed.

"Oh, it's the same thing," Pearl dismissed.

"Ma, you can't say that 'cause it's not the same thing," Evelyn scolded. "That's borderline racist."

"I'm not racist," she countered. "I love the gays."

"That's not the same thing...at all," Evelyn's husband, Chaz, mumbled to himself as he held back a chuckle.

"See what I mean? Conservative and not at all politically correct," Cal murmured to Sophie. "It's easier if she doesn't know."

"Anyway, so are you or are you not a Mexican?" Pearl continued.

"No, I'm mostly Greek," Andrew informed her.

"Oh good!" she replied.

"Hey, Andrew, I'm Tom," Cal's other uncle introduced. "Let me apologize in advance for having to deal with us crazy bastards. You're a brave man."

"Ha ha, I'm happy to be here," Andrew laughed. "I'm glad to finally meet Claire's family."

"Well, get through dinner and then tell me if you still mean that," Tom joked.

"Oh, hello, hello, hello," Mrs. Adams greeted with glee as she entered the cluttered foyer. "Come in, everyone. We've got drinks in the family room."

"Finally, the one good thing about the holidays," Cal murmured to Sophie. "I know how I'll be getting through today."

The clan made their collective way into the family room, where they continued to mingle over drinks and appetizers. The majority of the discussion leaned toward Claire and Andrew, as the family gently meddled to learn more about their relationship. Mrs. Adams—who popped in and out of the toasty kitchen to check on dinner—made the obligatory rounds as hostess to socialize with her relatives and freshen their drinks. After about an hour or so, she announced it was time for gifts and the family gathered around for their classic Secret Santa exchange.

Just after four o'clock, Mrs. Adams declared dinner was ready and instructed everyone to bring their drinks into the dining room. The family seated themselves at the decorated table as platters of succulently braised ham, seasoned vegetables, and fluffy mashed potatoes were served along with other side dishes. Plates were loaded with delicious food, glasses were filled with various liquors and mixers, and conversations stifled as everyone chowed down on the feast that Mrs. Adams had slaved over.

Despite all that had occurred over the past few days, Cal was beginning to enjoy himself. Although he had been glum and frustrated earlier that day, it was difficult not to enjoy oneself on Christmas—especially when in the company of family, which Cal certainly reveled in. As dinner came to an end, he assisted his mother in clearing the table and soaking the used dishes in the sink. Once they were finished, Mrs. Adams put on a pot of coffee, and Cal poured himself another gin and tonic—his fourth—before he settled himself at the table next to Sophie. The family continued to converse and laugh merrily as they allowed their food to digest in anticipation of dessert.

"Thank you for dinner, Mrs. Adams; it was great!" Sophie complimented.

"You're welcome, sweetie. I'm glad we got to spend Christmas with you. It's been a while since we last saw you," she remarked.

"Hey, Andrew, you still mean what you said earlier?" Tom teased from across the table.

"Ha ha, I do," Andrew reaffirmed. "Mrs. Adams, thank you for having me this week."

"Of course! It was our pleasure," Mrs. Adams said.

"I hope we didn't scare you away," Mr. Adams laughed.

"Not at all," he replied before taking Claire's hand in his own. "I can't thank you enough for welcoming me in. My family is pretty small, so I've never had a Christmas like this before."

"Well hopefully this is only the first of many holidays together," Mrs. Adams said as she raised her glass to salute Andrew.

"Well, I think that's definitely a possibility. And I think this is the right time for this," Andrew smiled as he stood up from his seat, still holding Claire's hand. "Claire, these past seven months have been incredible, and like nothing I've ever experienced; I've never felt so in love before. Since the first time I met you, I felt such a connection with you.

"I have to admit, I was a bit nervous when you first invited me to meet your family. I know how much they mean to you, so I wanted to make sure I made a good impression. And your family is so amazing, and they've really made me feel like I'm part of the family.

"So, like your mom said, hopefully this is the first of many more holidays to come. Claire Adams," Andrew continued while he gazed deep into her sparkling eyes. He reached into his pocket and fished out a small box before he stooped down onto one knee. "Will you do me the honor of spending the rest of our lives together? Will you marry me?"

"Oh my God," Mrs. Adams gasped as she wiped her teary eyes. "Todd, did you know about this?"

"I did," her husband revealed as he beamed on his daughter.

"Andrew, I...I...yes. Yes!" Claire sputtered, and Andrew slipped a modest diamond ring onto her finger before the two kissed.

The dining room was overcome with joy as the family congratulated the newly engaged couple with applause and hugs. Mrs. Adams cried lightly from happiness, while Sophie tried to put on a convincing smile. Meanwhile, Cal chugged the remainder of his drink and then slammed the empty glass on the table.

"I'm sorry, but what?" Cal stated. "Are you fucking kidding me?"

The room fell silent as the entire family eyed Cal from across the table. Sophie squeezed his arm in an attempt to stifle his outburst.

"Cal, no. Not here—" she began.

"No, I've been quiet long enough," he stated.

"All right, Cal, what the hell is wrong with you?" Claire inquired harshly as she threw her napkin on the table. "Clearly, you don't like Andrew, which you've made evident over the past week. All I wanted was for you to get to know him, but I guess that's too much for you. So what's the deal? Don't you want me to be happy?"

"Of course I do, Claire. But you're not going to be happy with *that*—believe me."

"You are so out of line!" she countered. "You don't even know him!"

"Oh, I know him plenty well," he retorted, feeling a bit buzzed from both the alcohol and the chaos that was unfolding.

"What is that supposed to mean?" Claire demanded.

"Cal, quit it," Andrew said. "Not now."

"You had your chance," he said. "But instead you want to put on this little charade with that proposal and pretend everything is okay."

"What's going on?" his sister wondered, in a tone of agitation and confusion. "Did you two know each other before I brought you home?"

"Yeah, in the biblical sense," Cal quipped.

"From church?" Pearl inquired above the clan's shocked gasps.

"I've got a question for you, Claire," Cal said as he stood up from his seat. "Does Andrew still make that weird face when he finishes?"

"Calvin James!" his mother squealed aghast as she clutched her chest, and several other family members reacted with appalled expressions.

"All right, son, sit down," Mr. Adams instructed. "I think you've had enough to drink. Do you even know what you're saying?"

"I'm fine, Dad, and yeah I do," Cal said in his defense. "And I'm saying what I'm saying to save my sister from being fucked over by Andrew like I was!"

The table fell silent as inquisitive eyes fell upon both Cal and Andrew.

"Shit," Mr. Adams sighed as he recalled his conversation with Cal from earlier that week. "*Him?*"

"I don't get it," Pearl stated.

"Um...uh...ah..." Mrs. Adams fumbled, as she attempted to find the words to tell her mother.

"Um...Cal and Andrew...apparently they..." Evelyn began.

"They're gay, Ma. They're gay," Tom informed her simply before taking a large swig of his beer.

"Homosexuals! For the love of Christ!" Pearl clamored. "Martha, did you know about Cal?"

"Oh come on, Ma. You couldn't tell?" Tom questioned.

"Gee, thanks Uncle Tom," Cal said.

"We love you Cal, but you were never dating anyone. You never brought anyone around, so it was kind of obvious," he explained.

"Where are you going?" Evelyn inquired as Pearl got up from the table.

"Grabbing my purse," she answered.

"Ma, don't leave. Please," Mrs. Adams called in a shaky voice.

"I'm not. I'm just grabbing my rosary beads and holy water," Pearl said.

"Oh, Jesus, Mary, and Saint Joseph," Mrs. Adams groaned and buried her weary face in her hands.

"Andrew, what is he talking about?" Claire interrogated with tears in her eyes.

"Babe—"

"He's lying, right?" she questioned.

"Todd, say something," Mrs. Adams hissed at her husband, seeking some form of comfort or support in dealing with the situation unfolding at the dining room table.

"Cal," his father sighed, at a complete loss for words. "Cal, Cal, Cal..."

"Dad, I'm sorry, but—"

"Oh, you're sorry?" Claire spat from across the table. "Clearly, you're not that sorry since you felt the need to make up some lie that my fiancé is gay."

"Claire," Cal began, but his sister cut him off.

"I'm sorry that you're sooo miserable all the time. We get it; your life sucks—"

"Claire!" their mother interrupted.

"But do you have to always bring everyone down with you?" she continued. "Well, congratulations. You just ruined my engagement for me by pulling this stunt. Are you happy now?"

"Yes, Claire. I am *so* happy right now. Mom is crying, I just outed myself, Grandma Pearl is about to have the pope excommunicate me, and my ex is cheating on you. I am so fucking happy right now!" Cal shouted. "I didn't ruin your engagement; he did."

"Oh sure! Keep lying," Claire shouted in tears.

"Claire, he is a fuckboy. He is actively using a gay hook-up app."

"Bullshit!" she countered, feeling confused and hurt as she tried to process all she had been told thus far.

"Sophie and I caught him two nights ago meeting up with a guy he met online," Cal revealed.

"Sophie," Claire said solemnly as the family turned their attention to Sophie for an answer. "Is he telling the truth?"

Sophie flushed but nodded her head before staring down at her lap.

"Well, why the fuck would you wait till now to tell me...like *this*!" Claire snapped.

"Andrew was going to tell you, but then he pulled this shit like the fucker he is," Cal retorted.

"Language, language!" Mrs. Adams scolded.

"Goddamn it, Cal," Andrew finally chimed as he shot up from his chair and stormed over to his ex. "You want to act like some martyr; like you're protecting your sister or like you're some poor dating victim. But you're just as bad."

"The fuck I am," Cal retorted.

"Oh yeah? Why don't we see what Jacob thinks?"

"You don't know anything about that."

"I know enough. I heard what you two were saying at Crush," Andrew retorted as he jabbed a finger into Cal's chest. "You're just as bad."

"Wait, what were you two doing at Crush?" Claire demanded.

"The night that Sophie and I caught him cheating on you," Cal replied.

"The night after..." Andrew began; he knew he was going down and was not afraid to drag his ex along with him.

"Don't," Cal warned under his breath.

"The night after what?" Claire inquired.

"The night after we...well, why don't you let Cal tell you what we did."

Once again, the family gasped at yet another revelation.

"Cal, how could you?" Claire cried.

"Fuck you, Andrew," Cal growled reaching the emotional breaking point of their turbulent history. Cal clenched his fist and punched, striking Andrew in the jaw with such force that Andrew stumbled backward.

"Calvin!" Mrs. Adams shrieked in fright before the entire house fell silent. Andrew glared at Cal and wiped some blood from the corner of his mouth.

"I've got the holy water," Pearl announced as she reappeared in the dining room, "and I found some prayer cards too."

Without warning, Andrew charged Cal and tackled him to the ground. The two men rolled around on the floor, swinging punches at each other. To Cal, their kiss at Crush the other night was not their final goodbye; this sparring match was. He was finished with Andrew, and every strike Cal cast was to serve as an unfriendly reminder to Andrew that they were through.

There would be no unspoken truce or civility between the two as they had previously planned. Cal was hurt, angered, and embarrassed by that night's altercation, and Andrew was the root of his frustration; it had always been Andrew who was at the center of his troubles. Cal determined it was time he paid for all his misdeeds, and he punched his ex.

"Oh shit," Mr. Adams swore as he sprang up from his seat with Tom following closely to assist in breaking up the fight while the rest of the family buzzed in worry from the dining room table.

The two men attempted to pull the former lovers apart, but struggled to do so as Cal and Andrew continued to spar with each other. Meanwhile, Pearl clutched her rosary beads close to her heart and recited a prayer card aloud as she splashed holy water on the group.

"Come on, you two. Cut it out," Tom grimaced as he yanked Andrew by the collar of his shirt.

"Cal, stop it. Stop it!" Sophie cried as she scurried over to help Mr. Adams, who was pulling his son off the floor by his belt. After several moments, Cal and Andrew were wrangled apart, both bruised and slightly bloodied yet ready to continue their brawl.

"You're pathetic, Cal!" Andrew snarled. "You were pathetic back then, and you're pathetic now. You made yourself easy to play."

"Fuck you!" Cal barked before he wrestled himself free of his father's grasp and shoved Andrew harshly. "You're weak!"

"Hey, hey! Knock it off!" Mr. Adams shouted as he restrained his son.

"You're weak!" Cal repeated. "You put on this tough guy act and use people before they can see who you really are and realize you're nothing. You're just a little bitch; a little, slutty-ass bitch!"

Cal and Andrew struggled to be released from their captors' firm grip for a moment—ready for another go at each other—when a sob sounded that captured their attention; it was Claire.

"I hate you," she wept softly before raising her voice. "I hate you, Cal!"

"Me?" he asked in disbelief. "I was trying to protect you."

"Protect me?" she laughed in disbelief. "Look around at what you've caused. Good fucking job!"

"Claire, you're upset. You don't mean that," Mrs. Adams stated, and she wrapped her arms around her daughter.

"No shit, I'm upset. And I do mean it. I hate you!"

"Claire," Cal muttered as his flames of rage were smothered by a wave of guilt.

"Was I just some joke to you to both of you this whole time while you were screwing each other?"

"No, Claire, let me explain—"

"No, fuck your explanation! I hate you!" Claire screamed. "I hate you, and I never want to see you again. Stay the fuck away from me!"

"Claire," Mrs. Adams said as she grew visibly upset at her daughter's harsh words.

"I hate you!" she repeated.

"Claire," Cal said.

"Sophie, take him home," Mr. Adams instructed.

"Dad, I'm sorry—"

"I know you are," he replied. The conversation between father and son earlier that week seemed to have struck a chord of understanding and sympathy within Mr. Adams. Meanwhile, Claire continued to weep in the background as several family members attempted to console her. "This is just a mess right now, and I'm not sure how to handle it."

The scene in the dining room morphed into a blur as Sophie swept Cal out the front door and into her car. He blinked and was no longer in her car, but in his own apartment. Sophie sat Cal down on his bed and mentioned something about how she would pick up his things from his parents' house in the morning, but he did not really hear her because he blinked and Sophie was gone and he was lying under the covers of his own bed.

Time slipped by while Cal wondered how he ended up in his current predicament. While he lay alone in his dark bedroom, Cal's mind was still in his parents' dining room as that evening's events replayed vividly in his head. However—despite his public outing and surge of violence—one image stood out above the rest—his sister's pained expression.

"Merry Christmas," Cal whispered to himself as a lone tear trickled down his bruised cheek.

Chapter Fourteen

The aftermath following the Christmas Day fiasco had a profound effect on the Adamses, as interactions between family members were strained. Despite his parents' persistent calls, Cal attempted to sever communications with his family and only checked in when absolutely necessary. Feeling ashamed and humiliated, he sought isolation to heal. Truthfully, the only person he wished to hear from right now was Claire, but he knew that would not happen. Cal had always assumed the protective, big brother role, but this time his selfishness and lunacy had caused his sister's pain. He would never be able to forgive himself for this, and reasoned that Claire would never be able to forgive him either.

Fortunately, Cal had been keeping busy in an attempt to forget about the rift between his family. After New Year's Day, the gym reopened and incoming membership rates skyrocketed. However, there were still some housekeeping items to attend to at work despite the repairs and renovations. Therefore, Cal found himself clocking out of work later and later to get the gym back up to snuff.

Sophie was a great source of comfort during this time. She made herself available to hang out with Cal and avoided the topic of Christmas Day unless he brought it up. In addition, Rich—her boyfriend of over four years—

had finally proposed and asked Cal to be a groomsman, so the two friends occupied their time with wedding details.

Between work and Sophie's company, on the whole, Cal was fine. In fact, the silver lining of the holiday chaos was that Cal now had an optimistic view regarding the future of his dating life. Any previous emotional burden he had carried was released from striking Andrew, and he had received the closure he needed. However, a pang of loneliness would settle upon him every night as he went to bed—one that could not be resolved by a romantic relationship.

Cal missed his sister. He thought about contacting Claire, and even began drafting a text message once. However, he hesitated on reaching out and eventually dismissed the idea altogether. Cal knew she was livid with him and he could not blame her. So instead, he tried to adapt to his new life—one with limited family socialization.

That Tuesday night in late February, Cal was seated alone at a booth for two at Clive's, a local sports bar which he frequented. His glass of beer was half empty, and he swirled its limited contents around before finishing it off with a large swig. As he gazed at his empty glass, Cal dwelled on how he had let his family down. The guilt he experienced was so immense that he actually believed the young woman entering the bar was Claire, though her hair was shorter and styled differently. However, as she approached, he realized it was indeed his sister.

"Hey, there," Claire greeted sheepishly when she arrived at Cal's booth.

"Claire. Hi," he sputtered.

"Can I sit?" she inquired.

"Yeah. Of course. Sure," he stammered.

"Sophie told me you were here," she explained as she removed her olive trench coat and settled herself across from her brother.

"Oh," he said. At closer inspection, Claire's new, ombre hair was fashionable and made her appear more mature. "Um, your hair is different. It looks good."

"Thanks. After everything that happened, I needed a change."

"I can relate," Cal mused.

"So...how have you been?" she asked.

"Oh, you know..." he trailed off. "How about you?"

"About the same," she said and then hesitated for a moment. "Andrew and I broke up."

"Oh, I'm sorry to hear that," Cal lied, trying to sound sincere.

"No you're not," Claire stated without sounding accusatory before an uncomfortable silence fell upon the estranged siblings.

"I want to be sorry," he said.

"Don't. I'm not sorry we broke up," his sister revealed.

"Do you..." Cal began. "Do you mind if I ask what happened?"

"Well, there was a lot to process from...*Christmas*," she explained. "I didn't really know what to believe. But about a week after Christmas, I found some texts and pictures on his phone; you were right."

"I wish I wasn't," he admitted. "Claire, I'm—"

"Hey, babe, sorry I'm late. It was a little icy on the back roads," a man—with a tawny undercut and light-blue eyes—apologized to Cal.

"No worries. This is my sister, Claire," Cal introduced him as the man discarded his winter garments. "Claire, this is my boyfriend—Jacob."

"Oh, *Jacob*. It's nice to meet you," she said as she stood up and hugged him.

"Nice to meet you as well. Cal's told me great things," Jacob complimented. "I'll go grab us some drinks."

"Thanks, babe," Cal called after him.

"So...how long has that been going on?" Claire wondered once Jacob was out of earshot.

"That's a complicated question," he replied with a slight smirk. "We kinda saw each other a few times before the holidays, but didn't start dating seriously till after New Year's."

"So does he know about—?"

"Yep."

"How'd that go over?"

"Not so great, but we really talked it out and I was 100 percent honest with him...about everything. And luckily he gave me another chance," he answered. "Things have been good with us since."

"That's...that's awesome, Cal. I'm really happy for you," his sister beamed.

"Claire, I'm so sorry," Cal said. "I honestly don't know what I was thinking."

"Dad kind of filled me in on your backstory with Andrew," Claire disclosed.

"Oh," he replied flatly.

"Did you love him?"

"I think..." Cal started as he cleared his throat. "I think that I thought I loved him, but it's confusing. So much was going on in my life when I first met Andrew, and I think I clung to him because I liked the idea of falling for someone.

"But it was clearly the wrong time to get involved with someone, with me getting ready to graduate and move away—especially when that person was Andrew. But I fell for him and got attached. I mean, I lost my virginity to him and that was the last memory I had of us...and all those bottled up emotions...and then to see him after all these years...

"I think I thought I was still in love with him, from when I was in college, except now I realize I was never in love with him. And now it's like I can think so clearly after years of being hung up on something so insignificant. And now that I'm saying all this out loud, I feel stupid and foolish—"

"You're not stupid. I understand what you're saying," Claire interjected. "It's kind of ironic because I lost my virginity to Andrew too."

"Really?" Cal blurted out.

"Well shit, Cal. Don't sound so surprised," his sister laughed.

"Sorry, I didn't mean it like that," he apologized. The two grew quiet for a moment until Cal attempted to break the silence with humor. "You know, in college my fraternity had a name for brothers who slept with the same girl."

"Oh yeah? What?" Claire wondered.

"Tunnel brothers," he informed her.

"So what are we then? Tunnel siblings?" Claire pondered with a giggle. "Does it still count if a sister and her gay brother slept with the same guy?"

"Ha ha, I'm not sure," he chuckled.

"It's a pretty fucked up situation," his sister remarked. "Kinda funny though."

"I guess," Cal commented as he grew solemn. "Claire, I really am sorry—for everything."

"I get it. I know you were trying to protect me," she shrugged. "And I'm sorry too."

"But I didn't protect you. I should have come clean about us the first night you brought him home. Or at the very least, I shouldn't have brought it up the way I did on Christmas. I don't blame you for hating me," he lamented. "And above all else, I wish I could chalk up that night with Andrew to us being drunk, but I knew what I was doing. Like I said, I thought I was in love with him... He was right; I *am* pathetic."

"Fuck Andrew," Claire swore. "Well not literally, Cal. Control yourself."

"*Ha ha*," he replied.

"But honestly, he's an asshole," Claire reasoned. "You are not, nor were you ever, pathetic."

"Thanks, Claire," Cal smiled.

"And I could never hate you. You're my big brother."

"I know I keep saying it, but I mean it. I really am so sorry."

"I forgive you," Claire said and she gave Cal's arm a gentle, reassuring squeeze. "Just promise me you'll never sleep with any of my future boyfriends again."

"Well then don't take my sloppy seconds," he teased. "You bitch."

"I mean it. Don't even think about going after Jacob."

"Ha ha, deal."

"Good because I can't be at the center of another family scandal. I don't think Mom's heart can take it," he continued with a chuckle. "I'm still not sure if I can show my face around the family yet."

"Oh, well haven't you heard? You might be in the clear because there's been a new family scandal," Claire informed him. "Apparently last week, good little Troy was busted at school with a joint and over two grams of something that wasn't oregano."

"Oh jeez, a homo and a toker? What is happening to Pearl's good Christian family?"

"Actually, Grandma Pearl is coming around," she revealed. "Since Christmas, she's been binge-watching *Will & Grace*."

"Great, so now when Grandma thinks of her gay grandson, *Will & Grace* is going to be the first thing that comes to her mind," Cal said.

"Better than Satan's hellfire," Claire joked.

"This is true." The two siblings laughed together, appreciating each other's humor after months of separation.

"I've got our beers," Jacob announced in a cheerful voice as he seated himself next to Cal and distributed the drinks.

"Thanks, babe," Cal smiled before his boyfriend leaned in.

"Everything okay?" Jacob whispered in his ear, aware of the divide between Cal and Claire.

"Yeah, we're good," he replied and kissed him on the cheek.

"Good. Then, what should we raise a cheers to?" Jacob wondered.

"To the tunnel siblings," Claire stated as she raised her glass to Cal's laughter.

"Um, what?"

"Just go with it, Jacob," Cal instructed as he raised his own beer.

"Well then, to the tunnel siblings."

"To the tunnel siblings," Cal and Claire cheered in unison.

About the Author

Rob Loveless is a corporate communications professional, who currently resides in Pittsburgh, PA. He has been an avid reader and writer from a young age, having been influenced by authors like Dan Brown. When he's not working or writing, Rob enjoys being active, exploring what the Steel City has to offer, and traveling.

Email: Rob.j.loveless@gmail.com

Twitter: @YepImLoveless

Instagram @rob_loveless

Also Available from NineStar Press

Connect with NineStar Press

www.ninestarpress.com

www.facebook.com/ninestarpress

www.facebook.com/groups/NineStarNiche

www.twitter.com/ninestarpress

www.tumblr.com/blog/ninestarpress